THE

LIFE

AND

TIMES

OF

HIERONYMUS ALOYSIS ZIEGE

BY HI ZIEGE
EDITED AND INTRODUCED BY JOHN BRUNI

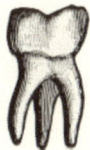

ISBN: 978-1-68510-051-3 (sc)
ISBN: 978-1-68510-052-0 (ebook)

First printing edition: June 24, 2022
Printed by Bizarro Pulp Press in the United States of America.
Cover Design and Layout: Don Noble
Edited by Nick Day
Proofreading and Interior Layout by Scarlett R. Algee

Bizarro Pulp Press, an imprint of JournalStone Publishing
3205 Sassafras Trail
Carbondale, Illinois 62901

Bizarro Pulp Press books may be ordered through booksellers or by contacting:

JournalStone | www.journalstone.com

THE
LIFE
AND
TIMES
OF
HIERONYMUS ALOYSIS ZIEGE

INTRODUCTION
BY JOHN BRUNI

NOT MUCH IS known about Hieronymus Aloysis Ziege. In fact, until recently the only mention of him, and it's not even by name, is in the journal of one William Clark, the second in command of the famed Lewis and Clark Expedition, formally known as the Corps of Discovery Expedition. This manuscript, for a couple of hundred years, remained in the attic of Zebulon Ziege, the many greats-grandson of HA Ziege. It shocked historians for its honesty and its vulgarity. It was also very difficult to read due to language at the time and Ziege's near-illiteracy.

When this story fell into my lap, I had no choice but to research more. I read both Lewis and Clark's journals for more clues as to the mysterious and fascinating HA Ziege, but all I could find was that one non-name mention. To quote Clark, who was only slightly more literate than Ziege, "That ugly idjit we met in La Charrette tuk a pistle and shot that bear in de face pointe blanke." Nothing more is said about "that idjit" in any other text.

Until now.

I have, for the sake of readability, updated Ziege's language and cleaned it up as much as I could without losing his voice. I hope I have been successful in this endeavor. I try not to write long introductions, so without any further ado I move the curtain to the side and let Hieronymus Aloysis Ziege take the center stage.

CHAPTER ONE

MY NAME IS Hieronymus Aloysis Ziege. People call me Hi, so feel free to do so, too. I don't know when I was born because Pa didn't know how to read or write, so he wasn't too good at keeping records. I figure I'm nearing eighty or ninety now, and I'm no prettier'n when I was a lad. Pa says that my mom was a goat, which is probably why I'm so damn ugly. I have a long face with Pa's blue eyes sunken into it and a long nose and teeth that look like a crooked picket fence. Them teeth're strong, though. I could probably bite the lid off a tin can. I guess that was Ma's contribution to my looks.

I'm tall and skinny with a nest of hair at the top of my head thicker than wool. It used to be pure black, like Pa's, but of recent years it's been getting more white in there than black.

I have two older brothers, both also born from goats. One of 'em, Cephus Ziege, left home before I was born. He fell face first into a bear trap. If he hadn't put his hand up, he probably would have lost most of his face. Instead, he lost a hand and the tip of his nose and chin. According to Pa he didn't look very pretty in the first place, so it was no skin off his...well, you know. After he healed, he headed off for parts unknown.

The other was Jebediah Ziege. He was only two years older than me, and he looked just like me and Pa: ugly as sin. Which was odd because Pa was big into Bible teaching. He couldn't read a lick of scripture, but he trusted what the preacher said every Sunday. I could read as a kid, but I never bothered to mention the part where man should not lay down with animals. That'd plum break his heart, and despite the beatings, I loved Pa. So did Jeb. He could read a little, too. Not as good as I could, but he knew the same part of the Bible I'm talking about here.

Jeb and I grew up real well, with Pa teaching us everything we needed to know about living off the land. We planted crops at the edge of the known continent. Known to white people, of course. There were Kiowa further west, and they knew a lot about the land, so I guess it's stupid saying that we were at the edge of the known continent. Kind of like saying that us white people discovered America when there were already people here. Pa didn't like such thinking, but I try to think things out for myself. Jeb was not like that. He loved Pa too much to be his own person.

Anyways, I could shoot the dick off a fly at fifty paces by the time I was eight. I'd dressed my first deer by nine. I'd taken down my first bear at eleven. I tell you, we were great at hunting. Like the Kiowa, we used everything of the animal. Nothing went to waste. None of us liked killing, so we respected our targets. Let me tell you, we were never short on skins. We did a lot of trading with the Frenchmen down from Quebec. I guess we were pretty wealthy for a group of ugly farmers in the middle of nowhere.

We also had some livestock. Beef, chicken, pork, we had it all. We sold a lot, but most of it was there to keep us fed. Pa particularly liked eggs, so we didn't sell many of those. Eggs were nice and soft, so he could get those down well. When he was fifteen a horse kicked him in the face. It was a shock to all that he'd survived, but he lost most of his teeth. A barber fixed him up with a set of falsies clipped to his remaining teeth, but those were also pretty bad. I learned some dentistry by helping Pa out with those things. After a while the fake teeth wouldn't clip in anymore, so Pa sent away for a mail order set that fit all right, provided he didn't eat anything.

Pa's mouth hurt a lot, so whenever he went to town, he picked up a case of whisky. Real rotgut, too. Nothing with a label on it. He drank a lot. Sometimes he didn't get out of bed unless he'd had at least a couple of gulps. That steadied him for working the land. It also inspired more than a few beatings. He didn't like to beat us, but he said it was for our own good. Jeb bought that hook, line, and sinker, but I always wondered about that one. You'd think that if something was good for you, it wouldn't hurt quite so much. He usually used his belt, but when it wasn't handy, he got pretty creative. One time he lashed us with a length of barbwire. It tore out the seats of our pants, but it didn't really hurt as bad as one would expect.

I learned a few other things from Pa, like some horse doctoring. I got some person doctoring in, too, when Jeb accidentally shot his big toe off his right foot. He'd wanted to wear a pistol on his hip, like he saw some people in town do. He wasn't paying attention, and the minie ball fired into his foot. I sewed him up pretty good. I'm good at sewing, too. I'm good at a lot of things. I even have some people skills. I'm good at making friends and talking and such, so I was welcome in town whenever we came looking for supplies or to trade. Pa left me in charge of that so he could go to the saloon. Usually, he rode in the back of the wagon when we left, too drunk to do anything else. I'd also drag him into the house and to bed on those occasions.

Not everything that happened to us back then was good and carefree, though. The Kiowa liked to keep us on our toes by raiding the farm. Sometimes cattle went missing. During one harvest season we lost a third of our corn crop mysteriously. Once they tried to get our chickens, but Pa shot two of 'em (the Kiowa, not the chickens), and the rest ran away. We got into the occasional skirmish with them, and we usually won. One time they tried to burn us out by setting our roof on fire, but we were prepared for such things, and it didn't work. They gave up trying to put one over on us after a while, and all was quiet after that.

We also got our share of bears. Usually one of their young 'uns would wander too close to our house, and the mama bear went crazy on us, thinking we were trying to hurt her cub. We steered clear whenever we could, but once Pa got too close and caught a claw to his chest. It wasn't too deep, thankfully, and I was able to sew him up good. He had a fever for a while, but I kept watch over him while Jeb worked the farm.

Eventually Pa's drinking got the better of him, and he started letting things go in favor of the bottle and the Bible. He'd sit in his favorite chair pretending to read the Good Book while sipping at a bottle of his rotgut. There were some pretty pictures in there, though, so he looked at those a lot. When he wanted to really read something, he'd pretend he'd lost his reading glasses—which he didn't own—and would ask me or Jeb to read to him. But mostly he was in his own world, probably thinking about better days. Maybe thinking about Ma.

Things started going wrong for the farm. Crops wouldn't grow right. The animals were malnourished. We suddenly had a tab at the town mercantile and livery. I didn't know what to do, and Pa wasn't much help. Jeb wasn't as smart as me, so he thought it would all blow over.

It would not.

Pa found a new love: one of the goats in our stable. Said she looked a lot like his Mabel, which was Ma's name. Called this one Viola. Viola started living inside with us, and at night I covered my ears because Pa's passion could be very loud. Jeb usually listened, wondering when he would find true love with a goat. I told him we should probably find human women to be our wives, but Jeb was dead set against it. He wanted a goat for his bride.

One night over dinner, Pa announced that he and Viola were going to get hitched. He wanted me to do the hitching for them, since I could read best. I told him that maybe this wasn't the way to go, but he insisted. He also wanted me to do it then and there, right after dinner. Just to shut him up, I said I'd do it.

We all dressed in our Sunday finest, which wasn't too fine for any of us, really, but it was the best we had. We didn't have any rings, but Pa said that was fine. They didn't need symbols to dictate their love for one another. He thrust the Bible in my hand and told me to find the marrying part.

I was sure the marrying part wasn't in the actual Bible, but I made it up as I went along. I'd been to a couple of weddings, and I thought I had the important parts down pretty well. As it turned out, Pa had no idea one way or the other, and when I reached the end of my remarks, he kissed Viola more passionately than I'd ever seen before. I turned away, and I was lucky. That was when Pa decided to consummate the marriage right in front of us. I trailed away, trying to get Jeb to come with me. He stayed, though. He wanted to know what to do on his own wedding night.

Not too long after that, we all noticed that Viola was getting slightly bigger. Pa said that she was pregnant with one of our siblings. I exchanged a glance with Jeb, but he didn't seem to think anything was amiss. I smiled and nodded just to get along.

Then came the night Viola went into labor. Pa had a lot more years on me, but I was the best when it came to birthing livestock. He said I had a midwife's touch. I agreed to help Viola push out her offspring, and when it happened, it kind of surprised me. I'd thought Pa's talk about our Ma being a goat was kind of silly, but maybe he wasn't lying. The baby that came out looked a lot like us. It had more of a goat's body, but the face was all Ziege.

It didn't survive more than two minutes. Viola hadn't survived, either. Pa cradled his first daughter in a blanket for a while, crying and drinking from his whisky bottle. He rocked her like she was still alive, but when he saw it had no effect he sighed and placed the baby next to her mother.

Jeb and I buried them both out by Mabel. Pa was unable to make the services, so we just said a few quick words before shoveling dirt over them. Jeb, who was very good at drawing, made a couple of wooden markers for them with doodles on them, signifying what they'd been in life. Viola's had an image of a goat wearing a dress, and the unnamed daughter was depicted with a baby Ziege wrapped up in a blanket.

Pa was inconsolable after that. He didn't even pretend anymore. He started every day with a swallow of whisky, and he kept it up through until well after the sun set. He never left his bedroom, which had taken on the stink of booze farts. When he could speak, he would talk about how good he would have been with a daughter. He'd always wanted one to go with his boys. His clear blue eyes, just like mine and Jeb's, wept constantly. Well, we didn't weep. Pa did. Our eyes are just the same, is all I was trying to say.

Since Pa removed himself from working the farm, conditions got better. We were no longer in debt. Our crops got better, and our animals looked a lot sturdier. Jeb and I were very good at taking care of things while Pa fell apart in his bedroom, screaming and crying sometimes, always drunk, never remembering anything. We thought his skin would eventually go yellow, and we'd lose him to the bottle forever.

Oddly enough, that didn't happen. Something else got Pa first.

CHAPTER TWO

I'LL GET BACK to that in a moment. Right about then I started feeling like an adult. I had been going to town to the saloon for a while, probably starting when I was fifteen, although since I don't know when I was born, you'll have to take that as an estimate. I also stole a few nips from Pa's whisky when he was passed out beyond all reason. I didn't turn into a drunkard and was certainly not anywhere near Pa's league, but I fancied a drink here or there. I preferred something at least a level above rotgut, but sometimes rotgut was the perfect thing to sip on, depending on your situation.

Jeb had been feeling all growed up for a time before my advancement. He did a lot of adult things, but he was always ready to go to work on the farm the next day. I decided I was too old to be jerking off, so I finally went to town when no one was looking. I stopped in at one of the two saloons they had, and I said to the bartender that I was interested in finding out about sex.

"You came to the right place," he said. Old Louise came down the bar to me and introduced me to a brand new world. I must have blown my load three times in that first hour before I could last longer than five minutes. Over the years she taught me a lot more than most people ever learn. Of the three local whores, she was my favorite, and we always had a lot of fun together.

Old Louise wasn't really all that old. She had to be no more than forty years of age. Some would call her fat, but all her curves were in the right places. She told me that when she'd started out in this game, she had tiny titties. By the time I got to her, age had made them blossom. Same for her ass. I can't tell you how many times I kissed the dimples on her bottom, and when we finished, she sometimes let me use her ass as a pillow. Those cheeks were perfect.

Sometimes she was already with a client, so I had to go to one of the others. I got to show off what I'd learned from Old Louise. I made them all cum. They'd tell me how good I was at this, and it didn't help that I had (and have) a pretty big dick. I'm not bragging. It ain't bragging if you're telling the truth.

It got to the point where I picked a lady for the night, and the others would get all sad-like. I tried to be fair and switch up each visit. After, they would tell me about how there were some men in the area that turned their stomachs, but they couldn't turn down that business. They were glad to see me. Old Louise taught me to never forget about one's partner's desires, and that I should see to them, sometimes before my own. I never forgot that lesson, and I practice it to this very day.

Yeah. I still fuck. I'm randy as all get out.

I got to be quite the man about town after that. One develops a reputation as a whore-hopper, but I was so nice about it that regular folks didn't mind seeing me one bit. In fact, some looked forward to meeting with me, especially the old fella at the general store. The Ziege farm was doing so well back then we could afford plenty of supplies, and we lent out some whenever we could. There were a lot of folks who weren't doing so well, so why not share the good times? It only seemed fair.

One day I took a peek into Pa's room to see how he was doing. It was a wet day outside, so there wasn't much we could do to work the farm at the time. When I saw the state of his ceiling, I knew it had to be repaired. It looked yellow with a bit of a purple patch smeared through the middle. Every so often water would drip down on Pa's bed. It usually missed him, but it couldn't be very comfortable. With Jeb's help, I pushed the bed to the side. Pa didn't so much as twitch. I put a bucket under the ugly stain, and we could hear water drop into it from all the way across the house.

It stopped raining two days later. I checked the Farmers' Almanac, and it said it wouldn't rain again for at least a week. I let the house dry off for a couple of days, and then I went up a ladder with a hammer hooked to my pants, a set of nails in my mouth and a thin piece of wood. It looked worse up here. There was almost a hole through the roof. I placed the sheet of wood over the entirety of the damage and started pounding nails into place.

I got two of them in before the roof collapsed. I fell clean through it, thankfully dropping the nails in my mouth. I landed all crooked, and it took me a moment to figure out why. If I hadn't moved Pa's bed, I would have landed full on top of him. As it was, only half of the mess landed on top of him. While I just had a couple of bruises and scratches, Pa had his head crushed like a melon. To add insult to injury, the hammer came down claw first into his chest, directly into his heart. Talk about bad luck.

I still dragged the wood off of him and checked for breath. There was none, and he didn't have any blood pumping through him. At the very least, he went out mashed to the gills.

Jeb had heard the racket, and when he saw what remained of Pa, he broke down crying. I probably would have cried, too, if not for the utter pain I felt from falling through the roof. It took us both some time, but we wrapped him up in his blanket like one of them Mexican sandwich rolls and buried him out by his beloved goats and his daughter. I said a few words over the grave, making them up like last time. I couldn't find the Bible, but I did have the Farmers' Almanac. Jeb could kinda-sorta read, so I worried that he would catch me, but he hardly looked over during the ceremony.

Shortly after, we patched up the roof from a lot more materials than I had been planning. Soon we cleaned out Pa's room so we could both have our own rooms. We lasted for a while like that, working the farm as best we could, which was pretty good. We had a lot of money at the time, but I felt lost working the land that Pa cared so much about before he became a drunkard. I felt...bored, I suppose would be the proper word. Mostly I just didn't want to be there anymore, and town was a bit too small for my likes.

I took Jeb aside and told him we should sell the farm and move west. There had to be bigger and better opportunities out there. He recoiled with shock when I'd suggested such a thing. He got angry with me and yelled a lot. At the time I thought he was still grieving Pa (and I am, too, to this very day), but I also suspected he was a bit afraid of leaving what he'd known forever. I loved Jeb. I went to his funeral a couple of years ago. Thankfully he had a wife and children to take over the farm, one of his sons a healthy and hardy young man. I didn't want to sell the place, but I would have if they hadn't been there.

Back when it was just Jeb and me, though, I had the farm appraised. We each had our own money, and I sold him my half of all the property. I kept two horses, one to ride and the other to carry my belongings. I stopped off at Pa's grave and said a few words like he'd still been alive. I also said a few words to the dead goat who was supposed to have been mine and Jeb's Ma. I still didn't buy it, but I thought it would be rude to say nothing.

I headed west to a town called La Charrette, which was supposedly the last town on the frontier. It was, for white people. There were plenty of tribes west of there with their own towns. La Charrette sounded like just the place for a young traveler like me to go, so I went.

CHAPTER THREE

LA CHARRETTE WAS a small place, but it always seemed busy to me. You could probably toss a dead rat from one end of town and out the other, it was that small. Since the Missouri flooded there often, we always had wooden planks going from boardwalk to boardwalk. When it got tougher to navigate, we didn't bother, unless we had a horse.

I had a lot of money, even by today's standards, so I got a nice room at the best hotel they had. Actually, it was the only hotel they had, unless you counted the boarding house at the north end of town. No one did, since they were full up, and it was the kind of place you might wake up with your throat slit, or if you were lucky, you just couldn't find the money you know you had the night before.

I stayed in the hotel where I led a fairly pampered life, all things considered. I even got to take a bath every day! I never got tired of that. I spent a lot of my time frequenting the saloons, but my favorite was a place called the Bloomin' Guts. It was run by a Frenchman, as just about every store in town was. I didn't know a lot of French when I first moved in, but after living there a few years, you pick it up. I'm good with languages. I can speak comfortably in my own (which I can't always say is true of my fellow Americans), French, Spanish, and I know enough Kiowa and Sioux with a smattering of Apache to be understood by a Comanche.

I spent the first couple of weeks getting shit-faced and getting pretty well known by the local whores. None as good as Old Louise, but they were pretty special. Worth every ha'penny.

I made some friends along the way. Jacques was this tiny man, not because he was born that way. He got his legs blowed off during the Revolution. He fought for the French, who I guess were allied with us at the time. Didn't even have no dick, just the stump of his trunk. He was hell on his hands, though. If he were in a race with a full-limbed man, I'd bet on Jacques. Never seen someone faster. He also played the piano at the Bloomin' Guts. When he got drunk, though, he turned mean, sometimes crazy. He'd talk about how his brother had been killed by the same cannonball that got his legs. He'd go on for a bit, kind of maudlin, but the more he drank and the more he talked, he got madder until he felt the need to "run" off into the night, vengeance on the mind. He talked about the murdering redcoats and how he was going to kill them with his bare hands, although the way he roared he could have been talking about "bear hands." By that point he was usually slobbering in a French accent, so it was hard to tell. Once I saw him headed toward the river, and it looked like he was going to jump right in and keep going until he hit England. I managed to grab him under the arms and bring him back to the saloon. I filled him up with more drink and put him on his piano bench. He still had some fight in him, so I turned on the player piano until it irritated him enough to put his own fingers on the ivories. His ability to plink out a tune was second to none. I miss that guy. I can only assume he died in a puddle of his own sick badmouthing the British.

I took to fishing sometimes for my dinner, which is how I met Sigmund. He didn't speak a lick of English, and I never really learned much about him, as he died three years into my life at La Charrette. We fished together a lot, and he caught a lot more than I did. I once saw him shove his arm into the river and come up with a catfish almost the size of a horse on it. He sold it to a local restaurant, and we all paid for the pleasure of enjoying its meat. He talked a blue streak, and I only smiled and nodded at him. He was tall, lanky, with a full head of hair that was so blond it was almost white. He couldn't have been more than twenty when we met. We shared some hooch from time to time, though he seemed to favor wine instead of whisky. Before my time, I'm told, he ordered red wine at the Bloomin' Guts. Someone tried to give him shit for it, and he clobbered the son of a bitch with one fist carefully placed on the jaw. Knocked the guy out so bad he didn't remember his own name.

One day when we were fishing, he got grabbed by the undertow. I watched him get sucked under, but I knew how treacherous the waters could be. There was no chance of me jumping in to rescue him. His head popped up once, and then something rose up from the river and grabbed him around the throat, dragging him down again. I'd never seen such a thing before, although I would later learn of octopi and their tentacles. It had been a tentacle—in fresh water, no less—and we later found pieces of Sigmund downriver. Something had been chewing on him for a while.

Then there were the twins. They looked nothing alike. Some called them Irish twins, although they were born on the same date in the same year. One had dark hair and eyes, while the other had blond hair and blue eyes. One stood at six-three, the other at five-five. One was well built, the other fat at the waist and under the chin. One spoke English, the other spoke English with a thick French accent. No one could figure out how Xander and Francois Becherer had come into the world. I learned from Xander that their mother had been a prostitute, and he guessed that she got knocked up twice on the same day. Didn't account for the French accent that Francois had, but what the hell? I didn't create this world. I'm just reporting from it.

I needed a way to show that I was making a living somehow, or eventually I'd get rolled for my money. Or they would ransack my hotel room when I was absent. I set about looking for work after two weeks. Thankfully I found it immediately at the hotel. They were looking for a night man. The job didn't pay much, but it did offer free room and board, and my meals were included. I still had a few coins for going to the saloon at the end of the day.

Someone found out that I had picked up some doctoring and dentisting experience, so they decided they needed a barber. I could handle the tooth-pulling pretty well and did so regularly. Most of my doctoring comes from looking at livestock, but I did all right at applying it to humans. I only ever had one patient die on me, but he was going to die one way or the other. He'd been shot in the head. He somehow survived long enough to get to me, but he was gone before I could even pull the bullet out of him.

I also got some requests for haircuts. I didn't have much experience with that, but I did good enough for my time in La Charrette. No one ever did complain.

Believe it or not, I also got some work as the backup bartender for the Bloomin' Guts. That one took a lot of trust, considering how much whisky I tended to down, but I guess I just have one of those faces. All right, maybe I snuck a drink here or there. If the owner ever noticed, he never said anything.

So, I lived and worked in La Charrette for a while. We rarely got visitors aside from trappers. They were the only ones who dared to go further west than here. Then there were the Kiowa. You never knew what you would get with them. Most times they wanted to raid town, loudly or otherwise, but a lot of times they were passing through, too. They just wanted to be friendly so they could get supplies they needed. Never did have trouble with the latter.

The constable was useless to us. He only had the job because he was the first to take up residence in the jail. He also found a tin badge that he took to wearing. He didn't really uphold any law. There was no law. We lived by our honor code, which not a lot of people had back then. La Charrette more or less behaved themselves. When they didn't, we never went looking for the constable. We settled our differences with guns if we had them and knives if we didn't. Sometimes someone wound up dead. No one ever asked any questions, though. We didn't have a bone yard, much less a caretaker, so the dead fella would usually go into the pig trough. We had no problem eating the pigs after that. It's the cycle of life. You learn about that kind of thing when you grow up on a farm. Though I'll be damned if the human-fed pigs didn't taste better than the others.

One time it was the constable who wound up dead. No one killed him. He just tripped on the boardwalk while supremely drunk and hit his head on the jailhouse where a nail was sticking out. Just dumb luck, all of it bad. The pigs fed well that night. They actually got drunk on the constable's blood and could barely stand up for the rest of the night. They all acted like they had hangovers the next day. We decided not to eat any of them that morning.

CHAPTER FOUR

I GUESS I'VE rambled on long enough. It's time to get to what you really wanted to hear about: the moment I joined the Corps of Discovery Expedition and the adventures that entailed.

May 25, 1804. When I woke up that morning, nothing felt special. It was just another day. Took my hair of the dog, just as always. Had breakfast at the restaurant that had the least rats living there. Took up shop at the barber's, where I pulled a couple of teeth before noon. Business as usual.

And then they arrived in La Charrette. Lewis and Clark, with twenty-nine other people. We'd heard about their expedition to the Pacific Ocean. According to the few newspapers we got all the way out there, Thomas Jefferson, the President of the United States hisownself, put this whole thing together. He wanted them to find a passable route to the Pacific Northwest. That was so we could establish a presence there before other Europeans could claim it. Meaning mostly the French, but the Spanish were also moving up, too.

Lewis and Clark were also supposed to take notes on what they find along the way and create amicable relationships with any natives they might find. Now as I think on it in old age, the whole idea of "amicable" went right out the door. I guess our subsequent presidents got greedy. Manifest Destiny, they call it. I once heard it called something else by a former sergeant in the army. He said it was actually just "killin' 'skins." I think he might have been right about that.

Anyway, the expedition was also supposed to take samples of wildlife and plants to send back to Washington City for studying. Jefferson also wanted a piece of the fur trade in the Pacific area. Fair enough.

He got Congress to cough up more than two thousand dollars. I tried to imagine that much money and couldn't do it. The number was just too big to fit in my head. The expedition also got a bunch of silver medals with Jefferson's face on it. They were supposed to be shiny gimcracks for the tribes to fawn over. I never did figure out for sure, but I suspect they were actually silver-plated. I find it hard to believe the United States of America would give silver away for free.

They also had one of the most marvelous things I had seen in my life up to that point. I have to admit that one of the reasons I chose to join Lewis and Clark was because I really wanted to fire that gun. It was called a Girandoni rifle. .46-caliber. That son of a bitch was a repeating rifle and could fire twenty times with force enough to kill a deer. You youngsters today have the Gatling gun, which is kind of the same thing. Not quite, but close. I eventually got to use it. I'll tell you about that later, though.

The main reason I joined up with the expedition was my wanderlust. I'd been a man about town for too many years. You ever see a zoo with a tiger? It's kind of like that, a big orange and black bundle pacing back and forth. You can tell when that bastard wants to eat you, that it's just trying to figure out a way to get through the bars. The world was out there, and I was hungry to see more of it. The only people we had come through were trappers or Kiowa, sometimes the Sioux. But this? The expedition? It sounded like a grand adventure, and I'd be a fool not to go with them.

They didn't come straight to La Charrette. They had camped outside town for luncheon. I rode out there on my horse and introduced myself to both Lewis (first name Meriwether) and Clark (first name William). I couldn't help but like Lewis immediately. I sensed an outdoorsman inside of him, and I later discovered that his childhood was a lot like mine, but with more money. Poor man came to a rotten end. Just about everyone said it was suicide, but does a suicidal man shoot himself in the belly? I think he was murdered, but that won't get you much more than a dismissive remark.

Clark, on the other hand...I never took a liking to him. He had a slight English accent, which grated on my ears sometimes. He was an outdoorsman, but not like me and Lewis. He had a cruel streak through him, like he killed for food but also for spite. The big reason I didn't like him, though, was the fact that he owned a slave. That was still legal back then. I didn't take kindly to people owning people. I never saw Clark beat his man, just speak loudly to him sometimes. York was the slave's name. He was a hale and hardy man. Apparently, Clark's father passed York down to him through his will. Clark's father had been the one to enslave York in the first place. I wonder how that happened. York never spoke of it, and it seemed to me that Clark never thought of it.

Clark, by the way, got to die of natural causes, whereas someone as good as Lewis was murdered by ne'er-do-wells in the dead of night. It's that kind of world.

I should also mention that I heard through a former expedition member that York asked to be liberated when the expedition ended. Clark, being the prick that he is, said no. He must have mellowed with age, because ten years later York asked again and was granted his freedom.

I wish I could have done that the day I met him. Clark never hurt him, though, and York seemed fine with his station in life. He didn't talk much, come to think of it. A revelation is coming over me as I write this part of my book. Did he not talk to me because he was not allowed to talk to white men without the permission of his master? If so, I am an absolute fool.

Well. I am a fool. All men are fools, when you get right down to the bone.

I learned all of that over the course of the years we traveled together, but I wanted my readers to know a bit about these men to get an idea of my first impression of them. I asked them if I could join up. They explained the purpose of their mission. I'd known most of it from the papers, and the rest I could piece together on my own. When I said I understood what I was getting into, they said yes.

They gave me enough time to run back to town and get my things. I spent some money on supplies (which included lots of whisky, as there were probably not any saloons west of there) and strapped them to my pack horse. I stopped by the Bloomin' Guts to say goodbye to the regulars and to hand over the keys to my barber shop to the bartender. The Irish twins were arguing, drunk beyond all reason at two in the afternoon. I only stayed long enough to say so long to the whores, who would miss my business and my cock. I found Jacques propped up at the piano. He wasn't playing it, though, just drinking. He seemed to comprehend what I was saying, as he was not too far gone yet. "If you see any British bastards," he told me, "shove a knife up their asses. Say it's from me."

That was the most English I'd ever heard out of him at once. I thought it prudent to make this promise, though I had no intention of sticking a knife into anyone, much less someone's butthole.

I got my pack horse and my riding horse, and I headed out to Lewis and Clark just outside town. Good thing, too, because they were getting restless waiting for me. At that point I took one last look at La Charrette. Even though I'd spent the last few months thinking of a way to leave, I thought I'd miss that little town. And I did, about two months into the journey. But I never turned back. I'd once seen the Atlantic Ocean as a boy. Now I wanted to see the Pacific.

And that was one big adventure after another. You'll probably call me a liar over what you're about to read, but I don't care. A lot of crazy shit happens in the middle of nowhere. If you don't go out and find it for yourself, you'll never know enough about your world.

Sit back and let me tell you about it.

CHAPTER FIVE

I WANT TO talk about Charles Floyd for a moment. He never stopped writing in that journal of his. He'd even write while on horseback in the middle of the rain. I don't know how he kept the ink from smearing in said rain. None of us had much more coverage than our hats or maybe a bandana. Chuck, we called him. Chuck could write backwards and upside down, probably. I think he could probably write in the middle of a battlefield, but I couldn't prove that, as we were never in a battlefield. I got a copy of that journal not too long ago and tried to read it, but he wrote them fancy words. The ten-cent ones. You know the type.

One of the few things I did understand was that he wrote of La Charrette as "the last settlement of whites on this river." He was right about it being the last settlement, but we saw some white people along the way. Not many, but enough.

By the first of June we reached the Osage River and a settlement of the Sioux. We didn't ride in to talk to them, which is what Thomas Jefferson would have wanted us to do. None of us spoke their language or their sign. Clark wanted to charge in there and take them by force, but Lewis, the smarter of the two, prevailed in staying peacefully away until we could find a translator. He sent several of us on different routes in search of French trappers, as they commonly knew the tribes in the area.

My group didn't find anything, but when we came back about a week and a half later, we found that another group had convinced Pierre Dorion, Jr., a trapper who coincidentally knew Clark's father well, to join our party. We rode down into camp and blessed their chief with one of those Jefferson coins. Dorion helped us trade and learn a bit about the territory. Chuck wrote ferociously that day. Never saw anyone write so frantically. It was like his ass was on fire and his dick was catching.

We got some excellent deer meat out of the deal, which the tribe prepared for us. They also did some kind of dance that Chuck detailed very well in his journal. I don't know how to make heads or tails of it, but it was pretty and they had lots of feathers. I enjoyed it quite a bit. The deer was exquisite. See? I know some ten-cent words. Exquisite. I like that one.

I discovered that I loved meeting new people. Sure, there were some colorful characters back home, but I was used to them. Seeing new people in a completely new place was exciting, and I got along with a lot of those we met, especially this group of Sioux. They invited me to smoke from their pipe, which I took to be very gracious, considering that their pipe was thought of as sacred. They had mighty fine tobacco. Better than anything I ever tasted from Georgia.

A word about Dorion: he was maybe the nicest French trapper I've ever met. Usually, they are smelly and rotten and think they're better than everyone else. Not Dorion. He was a very humble man, even when it came to his hunting prowess. Many times, after that Sioux meeting, I've seen him hunt. He was one of the best, and if he had said a few proud words about himself, he wouldn't have been bragging.

At any rate Dorion had us celebrating our new relationship with the Sioux. It sure was peaceful back in those days. Since then, the US government hasn't been too kind to their people. It's a shame. We did a lot to cement that friendship, and the people back east go and fuck it up royally. We could have done better, in my opinion.

Regardless of where the future would lead, the Sioux let us stay for a few days, and we celebrated the whole time. I broke out some of my whisky and shared it with them. They had never had anything like it before, but they sure loved it. They got pretty tipsy, as did I, but it was all in good fun. Dorion set it up so that they traded with us for another bottle of it. We got some nice furs and more deer meat, most of it smoked to jerky for preservation.

We left shortly after this, and there was a great ceremony where the Sioux gave us some gimcracks of their own, kind of like a medallion a soldier might earn in battle. We gave them more shiny things, and they seemed to like those. They asked about land east of there, and we told them about La Charrette, where they might trade for more whisky and such.

We went on our way, and on June 26, according to Chuck's journal, we made it to Kew Point, where the Kansas River joins the Missouri River. We didn't expect to see anyone living here, but there was a ramshackle farmhouse along with a stable.

We brought our boats to shore and decided to check out what was plainly an abandoned farm. As we approached the fence surrounding the house with the sinking roof, the front door opened and fell off its hinges. A white man emerged, hairy except for the top of his head. He cast his pale blue eyes around, surprised to see the bunch of us.

"Greetings," Lewis said. "I'm—"

"No," the white man said. "NO! NONONONONONONONO!!!"

"Excuse me?" Lewis asked. "I'm just trying to—"

"KEEP AWAY!" the white man screamed. He retreated into his house.

Lewis and Clark exchanged glances. Clark turned to York. "Maybe you should talk to him."

York glanced at the house. "I ain't going in there. That white man is crazy."

"NO!" the white man screamed from inside his house. "KEEP OUT! NO ONE IS COMING IN HERE!"

"See?" York said.

Clark scowled. "You're going in there, and you're going to like it."

The white man burst from the front door with a bulging carpet bag in his hand. "NO! WHITE PEOPLE! ALLOWED!"

Clark hooked a thumb at York. "He ain't white. He's my slave."

"WHITE PEOPLE RUN EVERYTHING! GO TO FUCK, YOU FUCKING FUCKS FROM FUCKVILLE!"

The white man ran west with great purpose. I didn't imagine him returning to his home anytime soon. Maybe ever.

"BLOW ME!" he screamed over his shoulder. He then disappeared into the woods until we could no longer hear him muttering curses under his breath.

Clark checked the stable. "No horses or livestock or anything."

Lewis sighed. "We might as well check and see if he left anything interesting behind."

A few of the men went into the house. Brave men. It seemed like it could collapse under a gentle breeze. I stayed outside until they returned. They didn't find much. Just a can of preserved jelly that could, conceivably, be turned into an alcoholic beverage. They also found an axe, but the head was on the rusty side, so they pitched it away.

We stayed long enough for luncheon before taking to our boats again, headed ever west. I wondered if we would ever see that crazy white man again. Only time would tell.

CHAPTER SIX

WHAT HAPPENED NEXT was, I am told, an historic event. It didn't strike me as such at the time, and it still kind of seems silly to me. What happened should not, in my opinion, have happened. I suppose in a way the event does serve history well, but we were in new territory. We didn't have any laws to uphold. There should never have been a trial. I have no problem with the crime that had been committed. But then again, I am reminded that the Lewis and Clark expedition was, in fact, a military force, so maybe it did need to happen. I don't know.

Our supplies were very well guarded. Well, I say "our" when I meant "theirs." My supplies I kept separate from everyone else so that I didn't seem to be mooching off the expedition. But Lewis and Clark were very particular when it came to said supplies. They made sure that someone was on guard at all times in all ways.

One problem: sometimes it is the guard who wants to break into the supplies, as it was in this case.

A word on John Collins: I didn't like him very much. He was always stand-offish or drunk, and he never really got along with anyone else. No one liked him, and even Clark called him a blackguard often and with great gusto. One time he came back to camp with pig meat and tried to say it was bear. Collins was in it for the glory, but sometimes he lost sight of that goal. He argued often and often lost, after which he'd scowl for days and ride drag for miles on end, not for any security reason, but because he wanted to stay away from everyone else. No one really trusted him except for Lewis. Lewis was a good man in that way. He trusted everyone until they gave him a reason not to. Very admirable in a leader.

Unfortunately, he trusted John Collins to guard the supplies on June 28. We all took to sleep early in the evening, hoping to get an early start before the sun came fully up the next day. Collins took up his position and remained somber as we all closed our eyes and drifted off. I fell off later than most, and the last thing I remembered was looking over at Collins to see that he was still in guard position.

Upon awaking the next morning, I discovered that everyone else was already up and frantic. I had no idea what had happened, but I soon learned from Chuck that Collins had done something extraordinarily stupid during the night. He had broken into the supplies for the sole reason of getting drunk. He'd taken down an entire fifth by himself and had been staggering through the camp. He accidentally stepped on Clark's head, and when he fell, his rifle discharged. Thankfully it didn't strike anyone. It roused almost everyone in camp, and they had clapped Collins in irons to prevent further tomfoolery. He was waiting to be tried for his crimes.

He had an accomplice. Apparently, Hugh Hall caught Collins in the middle of his night imbibing, and rather than report it, he actually joined in with Collins. He couldn't hold his liquor quite as well and was found passed out and stinking of whisky.

The trial of these two men, both privates in Lewis and Clark's Corps, lasted two days. There was a lot of argument back and forth, and none of it very controlled as we had no lawyers with us this far west of civilization. In the end Hall earned fifty lashes. John Collins, the instigator and leader of this insurrection, was sentenced to a hundred.

Have you ever seen someone whipped? I've seen it happen to slaves before, but never to white skin. Both kinds of men getting lashed are equally ghastly, but seeing white skin ripped to shreds like that brought it home a bit more to me. Ten lashes is too much, if you ask my opinion. Fifty is just ludicrous. A hundred is downright inhuman. Hall and Collins had strips of flesh hanging off their backs only to be flicked away with yet another lash. Blood ran down them in cascades. Soon their backs were one big scab. They stopped for Hall, and for fifty more lashes took out their vengeance on Collins's back. By this point it didn't even matter. The damage had been done so badly that this was just overkill.

When the spectacle was finally over, the medic examined both men. He cleaned their wounds with water and bound their backs as best he could, but blood seeped through the bandages almost instantly. Rather than waste more supplies on so-called criminals, they just put their shirts back on and continued the journey. Both men had red shirts within minutes of this. Everyone tried to ignore it, but it was simply impossible.

The men sagged when they walked to the boats, and while they each had very wet eyes, neither of them would allow themselves to weep, no matter how much they wanted to. They also had trouble breathing, and Lewis took mercy on them and said they didn't have to row that day.

We continued west, and when we came to another river Chuck notified us that it was the Fourth of July. We paused for celebrations. We didn't have much in way of fireworks, but we had firearms, and they finally let me shoot off the .46-caliber Girandi. All twenty rounds. It was spectacular. I even shot dinner for the evening: a giant seven-pointed deer. Even Collins and Hall got into a cheerful mood, what with all the fresh meat.

Sadly, such a good mood couldn't possibly last in the middle of nowhere.

CHAPTER SEVEN

THE BLOOD ON Collins and Hall's shirts wasn't even dry yet when we had our second wilderness trial.

A word about Alexander Hamilton Willard. He was likeable enough, but he was the laziest son of a bitch I'd ever known. If you told him to whitewash a fence, it would be done in several weeks' time. He'd be too busy taking naps and talking with passers-by to actually do any work. Lewis once asked him to mend his own saddle so he wouldn't fall off his horse. He fell off the horse after another day's riding, and only then did he get around to fixing the belt on his saddle. He was a miserable person, but when you got to know him, he was a good conversationalist. He'd had plenty of time to perfect the art while he was supposed to be working.

July 11. Lewis put him on sentinel guard duty. Clark called him a fool for even thinking such a thing, but Lewis was adamant about his trust in the man when it came to something as important as this. Willard seemed to be quite awake when the rest of us fell asleep.

When we arose the next morning, Lewis discovered that Willard had fallen asleep on guard duty. Not just propped up against a tree trunk snoring. No. He lay down on the grass full length and slept.

The trial lasted as long as the previous one had. I have to say, I've seen many trials over the course of my life, but I can't help but enjoy the ones where actual lawyers weren't involved. It felt a lot more honest. Not quite so much bullshit being flung into the air. It's kind of refreshing, even though by today's standards it would not be considered strictly legal.

In case you didn't know, sleeping on guard duty is commonly punishable by death. That's what made this trial so important. Lewis and Clark were both the adjudicators, just like last time, and after some lengthy conversation between the both of them, they decided not to kill Willard. Seeing as how they had a limited amount of men on this expedition, it would behoove them to keep as many of them alive as possible.

I promise you, Willard probably wished they'd killed him. Instead, he was sentenced to a hundred lashes over the next four days. At least that was decent. Not like poor Collins.

As soon as Willard was bandaged anew, we set off west for further discovery.

About five days after the final lashing, I was put on guard duty, which I took very seriously after Willard's piss poor example. Everyone except the guard on the supplies was asleep, and it was well into the night when the sky turned a curious green. I looked up to see an odd object hovering above camp in the sky. It looked to be maybe the size of a cabin, but it appeared like an upside-down teacup saucer. It shifted position and landed just outside camp. Armed with a revolver, I approached, wondering if I should wake Lewis.

York, who had been standing guard over Clark, came with me. "What the hell is that?" he asked me.

"I haven't the slightest," I said. I cocked the hammer of my weapon, all the same, and so did York with his.

A ramp extended from the bottom of the flying saucer, and a tiny figure emerged. It looked vaguely humanoid, but it was a gray color, and it had very big black eyes and a tiny mouth set under a nose made merely of two subtle slits. Some odd noise came from it, but it seemed to be adjusting itself to us. I felt something weird in my head, and when I turned to York, he touched his own head in the same place I'd felt it.

"Greetings, Americans," the gray creature said.

"Uh...hello," I said.

"We would like to speak with your leaders. The ones named..." Again, that probing sensation. "Lewis and Clark."

"I'll go fetch them," York said. Which was too bad. I felt really weird, and I wanted to go fetch them. But he called it, and I was stuck with the strange gray creature.

"I am Hi Ziege," I said. "What's your name?"

A buzzing sound filled my head, and I got the feeling that it was the creature's native tongue. "Or you can call me Al," it said in English.

"Al. Good. Very good."

Lewis and Clark approached with York at their front. Both men also wore their weapons, but they were not drawn and ready. "Lewis, Clark," I said. "This is Al."

"Uh...Al?" Lewis asked.

"Jesus fucking Christ, what is that thing?!" Clark nearly screamed.

"I'm from another galaxy," Al said. "I am an emissary for our people. They wish to make contact with this planet you call..." Probing. Probing. "Earth."

Clark drew his weapon. "I say we fucking kill the bastard. Let God sort him out."

Lewis carefully placed a hand on top of the gun and lowered it for Clark. "No. This is what we were sent out to do." He turned to Al. "What do you mean, galaxy? I've heard the word, but I don't quite understand it."

Al buzzed for a while, as if he were trying to figure out what to say to this. His big black eyes narrowed, deep in thought. Finally, he seemed to figure it out. "I come from the sky, far far away." Pointing up with a ridiculously long finger.

"So, you are from another world?" Lewis asked.

"Come on," Clark whined. "Let me kill it. We can preserve it and bring it back to Tommy Jeff when we're done with this journey."

At these words Al glanced back at his saucer, as if he were gauging whether or not he could make it to safety before Clark had the chance to blow his head off.

"No," Lewis said. "We must treat our guest with the respect he deserves. Please, Al. Would you like something to eat?"

"Eat?" Al asked. "We don't eat. We consume through osmosis."

"Osmosis?" Lewis asked. "What is that?"

More buzzing. Then: "We absorb our food through our skin."

"That's fucking creepy," Clark said. "Are you sure I can't kill this thing? Like, really sure?"

"William," Lewis said. He sounded like a parent about to scold a child.

Al looked from Clark to Lewis and back to Clark. "Maybe this wasn't such a hot idea."

"What do you mean?" Lewis asked. "Clark? He won't hurt you. I promise. I'm a man of my word." And he was, at that. I've known many men to give their word falsely, and Lewis never was that kind of man.

"I sense that you have a lot of weapons," Al said. "Something about a .46 repeater? That's a death machine."

"We are a scientific and sociological expedition," Lewis said. "We wish to study this undiscovered land and to make friends with the indigenous people who live here."

"But you have so many weapons," Al said. "You're conquerors."

"Well, no," Lewis said. "These weapons are for our protection. We can't guarantee that the indigenous peoples out here will be happy to see us. At least, not all of them. We made friends with the Sioux, and there is plenty of their territory ahead of us. So, we're not ruthless monsters."

More probing. At first it felt like a violation, but now it felt more comforting, like skinning your knee and having your pa take care of it for you.

"You are a man of historical knowledge," Al said to Lewis. "I'm not seeing a lot of promise in that history. You humans are much better at killing each other than loving one another."

"We've had our problems," Lewis said. It looked like it pained him to agree on such a point, but his grimace was short-lived. "We're working on it, though. Our journey is one of positive energy."

Clark guffawed, shaking his head. Lewis glanced sidelong at him, and Clark stopped.

"Yeah, no," Al said. "You guys aren't ready. I'll see you all in a thousand years or so." And he turned, headed back for his saucer.

"Wait!" Lewis said.

Clark raised his gun again and sent a minie ball into Al's head, splashing his insides all over the ramp to his airship.

"No!" Lewis yelled. "What have you done?!"

"Fuck this guy," Clark said. "He's a fiend, and he belongs in a giant jar on display in a museum. Besides, his airship is ours now. Think of the technology we could get from it. Have you ever seen a flying ship before? The most I have ever seen is a hot air balloon, and this thing is much more valuable than that."

Al's head came back together, and he spat until the minie ball came out of his mouth. A louder buzzing as he scrambled up the ramp, which rapidly closed after him. Clark frantically reloaded his pistol and took a shot at the airship. It only bounced off the outer hull, and the airship raised itself into the sky vertically and zipped away like a shooting star in reverse.

"Dammit!" Clark roared. He tossed his pistol down and flung his hat after it. "Dammit!"

"Why did you do that?" Lewis asked. He sounded more wounded than angry. "We could have made friends with a race not even of this earth!"

"Oh, shut up!" Clark said. He turned and headed back to camp. York followed with him, so it was only Lewis and myself.

"Al seemed like a good guy," I said.

"Yeah," Lewis said. "Clark is such an ass sometimes."

I nodded, thinking better than to verbalize anything. I resumed my guard duty, and when the sun rose again, we headed even further west. Just before dawn, however, I woke up Chuck in the interest of having a fully detailed account of our expedition. I told him of our encounter with the gray man and his flying saucer. Chuck wrote it all down furiously, making different sections for each of our accounts.

After Chuck got everything he needed, he set his journal aside. "So, you really mean that a...being from another planet landed a...a spaceship and tried to make contact with us?"

"I should have killed the confounded thing," Clark said. "I could have shown you the body, sir."

"Did you try the Jefferson coins?" Chuck asked.

Both Lewis and Clark gave him a disgusted look, each for different reasons. They both stalked off.

"I know what I saw," York said. He then wandered off, presumably to see to his master.

I shrugged. "It's all true."

Funny. When I read Chuck's journal later in life, there was no mention of the gray space man and his strange ship. I did, however, notice that the next day, Chuck had placed several journal pages into the campfire. I could only assume what those pages contained.

We moved ever westward. We met more natives, mostly Sioux. Somehow, they knew about us, perhaps from the previous village. We got a lot out of use from Dorion. We also got many gifts from our new friends. They really loved the Jefferson silver coins. Chuck got more material, and the rest of us were stuffed with elk. We introduced them to whisky, which one wit called "firewater." We made friends and got fabulously drunk.

And still we headed west, by boat if we could, on horseback when we couldn't.

The whipped boys eventually healed enough to do physical work again. "About damned time," Clark muttered. In his not-so-humble opinion, Lewis was too soft on these criminals. Clark felt that they had not needed time to recover, that they should have been put back to work immediately after their punishments.

I could only assume Clark had never received a single lash in his entire lifetime.

CHAPTER EIGHT

WE CROSSED WHAT would eventually be called the Platte River on July 21. Technically, though we had run into many Sioux villages, this was the beginning of their territory. We weren't nervous, though. Word of our passage traveled far and wide, and whenever we saw a new group of Sioux, there would always be a party.

What we found more concerning, though, was August 1. None of us wanted to do anything for this particular day, but we knew we had to do something. It was, after all, Clark's thirty-fourth birthday.

Begrudgingly, we threw him a party. There were some fireworks, so the night was lit up well while we all took turns firing the .46 "death machine." Clark got fabulously drunk and challenged Lewis to a jousting match. Except we didn't have the tools. It turned out that Clark fully intended to attack any challengers with his erect penis, held tightly in his left hand. Poor York. He's the one who had to deal with this sordid level of drunkenness. The next day Clark remembered nothing. His hangover held us up. He refused to budge until the ground stopped trying to slide out from under him.

A couple of days later we met two new tribes: the Oto and the Missouri. They, too, had heard of us, and there were no problems. Clark, still hungover from his birthday party, remained out of it, preferring to sleep under a lean-to. The rest of us had a good time.

Still, we had been free of trouble for quite a while. It meant it was only a matter of time before it reared its ugly head again.

When it did, it was in the form of Moses Reed. I don't know why he volunteered for this job. He couldn't be more ill-suited to this kind of expedition. He complained often about not having a roof over his head. He despised sleeping in bags and wanted nothing more than a bed. He missed home cooking most of all and would gripe for hours on end over the campfire food we had.

On August 4, he woke up groggy from drink and proclaimed that he was missing one of his prized knives. "I'll bet I left it at our last camp. I remember having it back then."

He asked permission from Lewis (not, I hesitate to add, Clark) to go back and retrieve this knife if he could. Lewis granted him this, and he rode as swiftly as he could out of camp.

It shouldn't have taken him more than two days to do this. He should definitely have been back by the third day, and we were going slow to accommodate his return. Yet he remained among the missing.

"You're an idiot," Clark said to Lewis. "You know what that asshole is doing right now."

Lewis sighed. "I fear you might be right. Still, he wasn't much good when he was around us. I think that being fooled by a lie is just the right price we should pay for never needing to see him again."

"Unacceptable," Clark said. "He needs to be punished. I'd be more than happy to go back and take care of this myself."

Lewis, good man that he was, knew what this would mean. Instead, he compromised. They would send George Drouillard back to retrieve our missing party member. George was a hardass. Likeable, but he was not very flexible. Clark suggested that George go, if that gives you any indication of the kind of man George was. Lewis agreed, and George followed our back trail.

We had another milestone while George went about his duty. Lewis turned thirty years old on August 18. Everyone was more eager to celebrate this than Clark's recent birthday. We held back on nothing. We'd kept the best fireworks for this occasion, and we killed several elk for a feast of epic proportions. Lewis, not quite the drunkard that Clark was, still drank, but he paced himself.

So it was that he was still fairly sober when George returned to camp. He had Moses in chains. He also had a new companion: Chief Little Thief of the Oto tribe. They'd met up halfway back on the trail. Having met each other during the Oto and Missouri party, Little Thief eagerly joined the trek.

According to George, Moses Reed was nowhere near the old camp. He was well on his way back to St. Louis, but he'd never imagined that Clark would send someone after him. Moses wasn't much of a fighter, so he surrendered himself without any trouble. George clamped him in chains, and that was that.

"Good work, George," Lewis said. "I'd be remiss if I'd failed to mention that I kind of expected you to bring him back dead. But this is very good."

"Not for Moses," Clark said. "Desertion is a hanging offense."

"Take it easy, Clark," Lewis said. "Let's not get out of hand."

Clark, ever stubborn, forced a trial on Lewis's thirtieth birthday. It brought a lot of us down, really. Not many of us wanted to go back to celebrating. The trial was short, though, and death was not the sentence, thanks mostly to Lewis. Yet I'm sure that Moses would have preferred death over what he did get.

"Moses Reed," Clark said, "you are hereby sentenced to run the gauntlet."

That might not sound very harsh, but let me assure you, it was. For the natives, running the gauntlet means you have to run past all the warriors in your tribe, who must do their best to beat and stab you. If you make it through, then you live.

Not so for the United States Army. To them it means getting five hundred lashes in one go.

York was ordered to chain Moses to a boulder, which he did. Clark checked the bonds, and when he was satisfied with their strength, he requested the whip. York didn't really want to do it, but he followed orders. I could see a clear grimace on his face when he handed the whip to his master. Clark took great relish in letting it uncoil and slap the ground.

None of us wanted to watch this barbarity. But we had to. Military rules.

Clark got winded after fifty lashes. Moses was still conscious and weeping, gritting his teeth. He didn't want to let out any screams, and he'd done a good job so far. He only whimpered when the whip hit him again.

Clark lost track of how many lashes at about two hundred and ten. He looked confused for a moment and wiped at the sweat on his brow. "Anyone know how many that was?"

All of us were painfully aware of how many lashes he'd meted out. York cleared his throat. "I think we're at two hundred and seventy-three."

"Oh. Good."

He resumed whipping Moses until he reached the count of five hundred. Out of breath, Clark put his hands on his knees. "Whew! That was an exercise!"

Moses was beyond hearing anything. His eyes were wide open, and his own breath came raggedly. No one was clearly at home in his body.

Clark gazed at the man's back. So much flesh had been flayed from it that we could see bone in places. I'd been pretty drunk at the time, but the mere sight was enough to sober me up. I kept swallowing so I wouldn't puke.

But Clark? He smiled at his handiwork. Rolling up the whip, he handed it back to York, who put it back where it belonged after washing the gore off.

"Moses Reed," Clark said.

Moses didn't even flinch at the sound of his own name.

"You are hereby discharged from your duty. Go from this place, and make sure I never see you again."

Lewis put a hand on Clark's shoulder. "Maybe we should let him rest a while, yes?"

Clark scowled. "No. He's a criminal. He should have known to expect this."

Lewis put a bottle of whisky in Clark's hand. "Let's have a few drinks first, then. Come on." He led Clark away while the medics went to work on Moses's back. There wasn't much they could do, but they did their best, and they gave Moses some opium to help ease the pain.

He was still looking pretty bad the next day, when Clark urged us to leave Moses behind. Lewis made sure to leave some provisions with Moses, including a sizeable amount of opium. Clark balked at this, but there wasn't much he could do about it. And so, we moved on west on August 19, leaving Moses behind. Moses followed us anyway—at a great distance, I should add—and he made it all the way to the Mandans with us. He helped build the fort, probably out of a need for penance. I think he got that in the end.

CHAPTER NINE

THE NEXT DAY, around one in the afternoon, we found a deserted village. Per Dorion, it was an Oto settlement, judging from the style of teepee and some of the furs still stretched and being cured. Our curiosity piqued, we took a look around. I found the medicine man's hut, but most of the items inside had already been plundered, probably by other Otos.

"Hey, check this out!"

It was York. He stood next to a tree, running his fingers along it. I arrived first and saw that a word had been carved into said tree. I didn't read too good back then, so I didn't know what it said.

Lewis arrived next. He, too, ran his fingers across the word. "Interesting."

"What, a fucking tree?" Clark asked. "Come on. Daylight's wasting."

"Croatoan," Lewis said.

"That's what it says?" I asked.

Lewis nodded, but he didn't explain further.

"What does it mean?" York asked.

"I'm not entirely sure," Lewis said, "but our country has an interesting relationship with this word."

"Yawn," Clark said. "Let's go."

"When white people first colonized this land, they created a village called Roanoke. They were fairly successful for a while. The first American was born there. Girl named Virginia Dare. Anyway, John White went back to England to run some errands, and when he returned three years later, Roanoke was abandoned, and there was no trace of the people who had lived there. All he had to go on were uninhabited buildings and this word on a gate post." He gestured to Croatoan again.

York cast a quick glance back at the teepee village. "Yeah, that sounds familiar."

"Lewis! Clark! You need to see this!"

Chuck approached us all, holding aloft what looked like a journal. He handed it to Lewis, who opened it and examined its contents.

"What is it?" York asked.

"It's a diary," Chuck said. "In *English*. Granted, it's awful English, but it is certainly unlike anything the native would write."

"Interesting," Lewis said again. "The style suggests a woman wrote this."

Clark offered peals of laughter to the sky. When he caught his breath, he managed to cut back to a couple of giggles. "Women can't write."

"Still," Lewis said. He showed Clark the contents. Clark, who could read maybe a little better than me, still guffawed.

"No, that's intolerable," Clark said. "One must not suffer a witch to live, and one must not suffer a woman who can write. I won't allow it."

Lewis looked sidelong at his partner, and then he turned to me, standing just behind Clark. I shrugged. I had no idea what to make of this.

"You think that the people who left Roanoke made it this far?" Chuck asked. "Because that would be very much of interest to me."

Lewis shook his head. "I don't know. Let's add this to the cargo. I have no problem in having the philosophers in Washington figure this one out."

"You want me to work on translating it to proper English?" Chuck asked.

"Sure." Lewis handed the journal over to Chuck. "See what you can make of it. In the meantime, let's see if we can find any unplundered goods worth taking."

That journal didn't survive to the end of the journey, by the way. We got stuck in treacherous waters farther along the way, and we lost a lot of supplies. One of them was that journal.

We worked our way through the empty teepees, but there was nothing. Clark, ever impatient to get moving again, suggested burning this place to the ground. "All the better not to think about it."

"Absolutely not," Lewis said. "All right. Let's mount up and get a move on."

For the rest of the day, as we journeyed on horseback, Chuck sat in his saddle and worked painstakingly on a translation of the mysterious journal. Sadly, he would never complete it.

The next day he stopped scribbling in his own journal. He stared straight ahead, a hand to his belly.

"You all right?" I asked.

"I just felt a sharp pain in my guts," Chuck said. "Kind of like someone just jabbed me with a blade." Then his eyes went wide, and he gagged back a scream. Doubled over in pain, he fell off his horse. I yelled for the medic as I dismounted and checked on my traveling companion.

"Chuck. What's going on?" I asked.

His skin went yellow, and he shook uncontrollably. He babbled, and I recognized a few words, but most of it was gibberish. Sweat glistened on his forehead as his eyes rolled back.

The medic—I can't recall his name for the life of me—went to his knees next to Chuck and started touching his stomach at random. "Tell me when I touch something that hurts."

I don't think Chuck understood, but when the medic touched his stomach in a particular spot, Chuck let out a chilling scream. I have never heard such a sound come from a human being, not even Moses Reed, and that is saying something.

The medic drew back. "Have you been feeling this for a while?"

Chuck was beyond answering questions at this point. All he could do was weep and scream.

"What is it?" Lewis asked.

"Bad news," the medic said. "His appendix burst. There's nothing I can do for him. All we can do is make him comfortable, to ease his passage to the next life."

Lewis pursed his lips. "Poor man."

Clark approached like a demon hell-bent on murdering someone. "What the fuck is holding us up now?" He saw Chuck and grimaced. "What did he do? Get into the whisky?"

Lewis's face turned to stone. "Chuck's dying."

Clark's features softened somewhat. "Oh. Hell. How long does he have?"

"Probably minutes," the medic said. "An hour at most."

"Get him the opium," Lewis said.

"We can't just wait for him to die," Clark said. "We're on a schedule, and so far, we're right on time. We have to move on."

"Have you no heart, William?" Lewis asked. I'd never heard him call Clark by his first name, and I didn't think that was good for anyone involved.

"York," Clark said. "I want you to wait with this man while he dies. When he has passed, give him a Christian burial."

"Sure thing, boss," York said. I thought I detected some sarcasm there, but I couldn't be sure. Clark certainly didn't notice it.

"Good," Clark said. "Let's move out!"

"I want to stay with him," I told Lewis.

"That's a good idea, Hi," Lewis said. "Catch up with us when you can."

I nodded and tied my horse to a nearby tree. I also hitched York's horse there, too. He and I sat down next to Chuck as the rest of the expedition moved forward. York administered opium liberally. Soon Chuck's whimpers turned to barely audible breath. York administered more.

"Isn't that too much?" I asked.

"Nope," York said. "I mean, it would be if we expected him to live."

It took me a moment to figure that one out. "OH!" I said. "Okay."

York gave him more, and soon that breath ceased, too. York held a mirror to Chuck's nose, and it did not fog over. I checked Chuck's pulse at his neck and felt nothing. Wordlessly York went to his horse and searched among his possessions until he found a tarp. I helped him wrap poor Chuck up like a cigar. We then worked at digging a hole. Not too deep. We didn't really have the time for a full six feet. Three was good enough, and we covered his corpse over with dirt, and then over the dirt a few big rocks to discourage any scavengers.

"You know the Good Book, Hi?" York asked.

"The good book? Oh, you mean the Bible?"

"That's the one."

I thought back to my sermon over Pa's grave. "Not really. Never took to religion all that much."

York nodded and stood next to the grave. He removed his hat, so I did the same. "We don't know any of the right words, Lord, so I hope this will be enough. Chuck was a good guy. He'll be missed around here. Take good care of him. Amen."

"Amen," I said. It seemed the right thing to say.

We mounted up, and about a mile away we found Chuck's horse. It no longer wore its saddle. As such, we couldn't find any of his belongings or any provisions that might be helpful in the near future. We did find his chronicles of our adventures thus far. I stuck it in my saddlebag. Same with the partial translation of the strange diary. I still feel bad that we lost that one to a river.

It really was a shame. I miss Chuck still.

CHAPTER TEN

THE NEXT DAY our scout came racing back to us after having ridden ahead for a few miles. Pvt. Joseph Field kept his horse at a froth as he rushed among us, searching out our captains. Finally, he saw Lewis and yanked his horse to a screeching halt.

"What news?" Lewis asked.

"You're not going to believe it," Field said. "You're going to have to see this for yourself."

Lewis, usually a patient man, also did not like surprises. "Just tell me what you saw."

"Remember how the natives told us about the giant animals out west? And we scoffed at the notion?"

"Yes," Lewis said. "I think they called it a bison, or something similar."

"They weren't kidding, sir. I just saw a pack of them ahead. You need to see this!"

"Lay on, Macduff," Lewis said. It sounded a bit fancy for me, so I could only assume it was a literary reference. I turned out to be right. Later that day, York told me that it was from the Scottish play by William Shakespeare himself. But I'd never heard of a Scottish play.

"That's not the actual name of it," York said. "If you say the real title, you're in for some bad luck." This struck me as odd, as York was not a superstitious person at all. I didn't press him, though.

Soon we came to a wide open plain, and sure enough there were giant beasts made, presumably, of thick fur and nothing else. We all stared at the pack in awe.

"I want one," Field said. "Can I please have one?"

"Well," Lewis said. "Finders keepers, I suppose. You'll want the .46, I take it?"

"Oh, yes sir."

Field dug into our armory and loaded the .46, lying on his belly to take careful aim at one of the bison. When he pulled the trigger, the explosion rocked its way through the environment, echoing tenfold across the flat land. All the bison scattered except for one. That one toppled over, blood spouting from its throat.

Lewis watched through a spyglass. "Very good shot, Private."

"Thank you, sir!"

We ate very well that night. Field also skinned the beast and started treating it like the Sioux had taught us. It would become two of the warmest blankets at winter, which was not that far off at the time.

The meal was so good even Clark kept quiet. No insults or challenges came from him. He was too busy stuffing his belly with bison.

Lewis, his chin slick with meat juice, turned to Clark. "You know, we should probably figure out how to fill that vacancy that Chuck left us with."

"You want to promote someone to sergeant?" Clark asked. He was barely audible since he spoke with his mouth full.

"Precisely."

Clark swallowed that wad of meat. "Who are you thinking?"

"I...I'm not too sure yet." But he looked at Patrick Gass. He was a private and a decent sort. He never really talked all that much, so I don't know if any of us could have counted him as a friend, but he certainly was no mountebank.

Sure enough, a few days later, Lewis and Clark came to an agreement. Just after dinner that night, before the whisky could get a hold of us, they made the announcement.

"Captain Clark and myself have decided that one among you has what it takes to fill the vacancy Chuck left us with when he died. We have decided on you, Private Gass. Please, step forward."

Gass stood straight as an arrow and stiffly saluted his superiors. They saluted back. Lewis then handed him a small wooden case. "Congratulations, Sgt. Gass."

Gass opened the case and saw his chevrons. "Thank you, sirs!"

As it turned out, that was the first election west of the Mississippi. None of us thought we were being particularly historic, but there you have it. I saw a lot of firsts as I traveled with Lewis and Clark, and I feel proud of that. I try not to let it get to my head, though.

Here's another first for you. A few days later we met with the Yankton Sioux. Dorion's translations weren't exactly perfect, but they were good enough for us to be friendly. As we traded pleasantries, a scream rang out in the night. Lewis inquired the chief about it and was told that one of the squaws was giving birth, and that the going was rough. The midwife ministered to the squaw, but there seemed to be nothing to make the birth easier.

"Let me have a look," Lewis said. We all followed him to a teepee with the flaps pinned open against the side. Inside we saw the pregnant woman, and the midwife crouched between her legs. Her lady parts were exposed to God and the world. That was the first time I saw a squaw like that. I found it very interesting that no matter what color the woman, the parts are more or less the same. I thought back to my time at the whorehouse and smiled.

And then I noticed something poking out of her lady parts. It was a foot.

"That's not good," Lewis said to the chief. "They're not supposed to come out that way."

"There is nothing we can do," the chief said. "So the Great Spirit dictates." He didn't speak English. We just got that from Dorion.

"I aided with many animal births when I was a child," Lewis said. "I think I can help with this. May I?"

The chief nodded and motioned for the midwife to step aside. Lewis took her place.

"This is probably going to hurt. Hi, you got that opium?"

"I'll get it," I said. When I got back, Lewis had already put his hand inside the squaw, who screamed louder than I've ever heard a woman scream before. It hurt my ears, which are pretty sensitive. Still are, despite my age now.

I administered the opium, and the squaw's cries faded away. She was barely conscious as Lewis maneuvered his other hand inside of her. It just about turned my stomach, and Lewis didn't look so good, either. Still, I'd done the same thing with livestock back on the farm. Just never to a human being, that's all.

"I think I got it," Lewis said. "Ma'am, I'll need you to resume pushing now."

Eyes dulled with drug, the squaw didn't seem to understand what was going on, much less what Lewis had said. Dorion translated for her, and she nodded. Grunting, she pushed as hard as she could. Loosened up by Lewis's hands, the baby came out swiftly, so fast that Lewis almost didn't catch it.

"I need a cloth!" Lewis said. "Someone help me!"

The only cloth I had handy was the United States flag. I looked at him, pointing. "That's what we got, Captain."

"Then give it to me!"

I took the flag down and gently laid it down between the squaw's feet. The chief stepped forward to cut the umbilical with a knife. Lewis then lowered the baby into the middle of it and wrapped the kid up like a bundle from the mercantile. He stood, cradling the baby and smiling.

"Look at that," Lewis said. "Now that's an American!"

I got kind of choked up. Didn't see that coming. I don't think Lewis was speaking with his tongue in cheek. I think he legitimately felt that way.

Considering how poorly the natives have been treated since, I think we need more people like Lewis in the world. He was a rare person who never judged a man by the color of his skin. That seems pretty smart to me, even now.

The midwife scooped up the afterbirth and carried it away. Lewis covered the squaw's nakedness and carefully placed the baby in her arms. Even though she was doped to the gills, the new mother smiled and whispered to her newborn.

It was pretty damned beautiful, if you ask me.

The celebration was grand that evening. We still had some fireworks, which we set off. After trading for the usual goods and sundries, Lewis presented the chief with one of the Jefferson coins. We demonstrated the .46, and one of the braves wanted to give it a shot. He fired into the darkness and whooped. The sounds of the night around us went silent. No wolves or crickets dared make their presence known. Not that any of us were sober enough to hit the side of a barn.

We stayed another day, most of which Lewis spent with the new mother and her infant. The whole experience fascinated him, I think. He smiled a lot and conversed with the aid of Dorion. The three of them got on like a saddle on a horse.

The dawn of the next day, we moved on. The next few days were not very eventful. It was more discovery than adventure.

There were a couple of notable things that happened, though. We were moving across the prairie when Sgt. Gass held up a fist, bringing us to a halt.

"What is it?" Clark asked.

"Did you see that?" Gass asked.

Lewis unlimbered his spyglass and pulled it to its fullest extent, gazing through it. "Where?"

"Aw, it's gone now," Gass said. Then he suddenly pointed. "What the fuck is that?!"

My eyes were very good, and I could see the object without any external aid. I saw a small furry creature poking its head out of a hole in the ground. At first, I thought it might be a weird rabbit, but there were no outlandish ears. It looked like a fuzzy potato. Almost as soon as Gass pointed, the animal ducked back into its hole.

"Get the water!" Clark yelled.

Drouillard, the man who dragged Reed back to camp for the gauntlet, rushed to the chuckwagon and dumped a bucket into the barrel strapped to the side. While he ran to the hole, three other men took the barrel down and followed. Drouillard knelt down and poured the entire bucket into the hole. He peered down, hoping for some kind of result.

"Move!" Joe Field shouted. He was among the three with the barrel, and as soon as Drouillard got out of the way, they poured as much of the barrel in as they dared. The hole overflowed, and the critter came up with it, coughing and wheezing.

"Get it!" Clark said.

Drouillard, who wore thick gloves, grabbed the little creature, making sure not to let its teeth get close to his fingers.

"Kill it!" Clark said.

Drouillard glanced up, a troubled look in his eyes. I felt it a little, too. Some creatures are just too purty to kill just to kill it.

"Goddammit." Clark dismounted and yanked the creature from Drouillard's grip. With one swift movement, Clark cranked the animal's neck, snapping it like a twig. He thrust the dead animal back into Drouillard's hands. "File it with the others."

Drouillard looked down at the poor animal, but he didn't argue. He followed orders. When it was back in Jefferson's hands, it was eventually called a prairie dog. It didn't look like a dog, but that science thing, bio-something-or-other. Who understood that, anyway?

Almost a week later Field, ever the scout, came back with reports of a new creature. He said that he'd shot the beast, and he likened it to a goat. He called it a "prairie goat."

I thought about my old man. I thought about who my mother was supposed to be, according to him. I thought about my stepmother. To say this didn't sit well with me was kind of like calling a horse a pony.

But then I saw it. It looked more like a deer than anything. We ate some of it and prepared the rest to be sent back with the prairie dog and other samples we collected. This one turned out to be called an antelope. I don't quite understand why, but again. It's bio-whatsis.

CHAPTER ELEVEN

THE FIRST REAL problem we had with the natives happened a week after the incident with the antelope. We'd taken to boats again as we traveled along what would eventually be called the Niobrara River. Joe Field, who remained on horseback, had ridden ahead and come back with a report of Sioux just upriver.

"It's like they're waiting for us," he said. "I don't know how they'd know we were coming, but that's how I feel it."

Clark checked his pistol. Satisfied, he holstered it. "We'll be ready."

"Let's not be swift to action," Lewis said. "We have had excellent relations with the Sioux so far."

Clark shrugged, but I could tell from the glint in his eyes that he'd been wanting to shoot a Sioux for quite some time. It was just the kind of man he was.

About a mile later we could see the Sioux standing sentinel on both sides of the river and in boats—they called them canoes—of their own. Like Field had said, they looked like they were waiting for us. My neck tingled, and that usually meant something was about to go wrong. I hated to agree with Clark on anything, but he could very well have been right about this one.

Yet still we approached.

One of the Sioux stepped forward and said something. He held up a hand palm out. We didn't need to know what he'd said. We stopped rowing. The tide threatened to move us, but we dipped our paddles in every once in a while to stay in place.

The Sioux spoke again, and he sounded angry. Clark's hand rested on the butt of his pistol. Lewis looked to Dorion, but Dorion shrugged. "These are Lakota Sioux. I only understand every other word."

The Sioux must have detected our confusion. He made several gestures and said a few words. He gestured at the boat in the lead. The one with Clark in it. I gritted my teeth and touched the butt of my own pistol.

"Boss," Dorion said. Not to Clark, but to Lewis. "I think he wants our boat as tribute."

"Tribute?" Clark laughed, and it was an ugly, savage sound. "We pay no tribute!"

Dorion rubbed his beard. "I could be wrong about that word. 'Toll' might make more sense."

"He wants us to give him a boat so we may pass?" Lewis asked. "Is that my understanding?"

The Sioux seemed to decide that Dorion was our leader. He looked to our interpreter and said a few words. Once again, he gestured to the lead boat. Dorion tried saying something, but the Sioux didn't seem to understand him. He made a gesture that looked a lot like a shrug but wasn't quite.

"Yeah, he don't understand me, Boss."

Clark looked from the Sioux to Lewis. "I say we shoot it out. They got spears only."

"One has a bow and arrow," Dorion said. "The Sioux tend to be good with those. We'd probably win, Boss, but they'd make us pay a high price for it."

Lewis glanced up at the Sioux. "I'm going to try something different. Hi, could you please toss me up one of the Jefferson coins?"

Clark grunted and shook his head. I went to the supplies and plucked one out. I tossed it to Lewis on his boat, and he stood on unsteady legs, holding the coin aloft so the Sioux could see it. Dorion understood and said a few more words.

The Sioux nodded and pointed to the riverbank. I had a good feeling about this. Even Clark let his hand drop away as we rowed for land. We pulled up just as the canoes did, and we faced the very small Sioux force. Lewis approached their leader and held the coin out to him. The Sioux took it and turned to his men, showing it off like it was a bar of gold. He turned then and tugged at Lewis's coat. It took Lewis a moment to figure it out.

"It won't fit you, sir," Lewis said. "Dorion, do you think you could at least approximate that?"

Dorion tried, and Lewis asked me to fetch a smaller coat from the supplies, which I did. I handed it to Lewis, who handed it to the Sioux leader. He donned the coat and smiled, showing off a set of perfect white teeth. He turned to the other Sioux and did an odd jig of a dance. They laughed, and the leader turned back to us. He pointed at Dorion's hat.

"Dorion?" Lewis asked.

Dorion nodded and doffed his hat. When the leader wore it, he looked slightly ridiculous. His men smiled when his back was turned, and I think we all had a difficulty in keeping straight faces. Even Clark looked like he was chewing the insides of his cheeks.

The leader now pointed at one of our horses. Clark snapped and drew his pistol. "We've given them enough! Dorion, you must demand our safe passage!"

Dorion looked to Lewis. Lewis said, "We can't afford to lose a horse. Offer him some tobacco instead."

I grabbed up a plug of tobacco, and before I could hand it to Lewis, the Sioux leader snatched it from my hand and put a piece of it in his mouth. He chewed it like it was jerky beef and swallowed it. He gagged and spat and threw the rest of the plug to the ground. Two of his men took to his side while a third moved toward the horse.

Clark whirled on him. "Touch that horse, and I will give your redskin brain a hole to breathe through!"

The Sioux paused halfway to the horse. By now the leader had recovered from his vile discovery of the dangers of chaw. He waved the warrior back to their side of our meeting. The brave obliged.

"It's fine," Lewis said. "Clark, you can put the gun away."

Clark did, but he wasn't quick about it.

The leader pointed to the head boat again.

"He can't have the boat," Lewis said.

Dorion sighed. "All right. I'll try something." He spoke to the leader again, and this time he incorporated a lot of hand gestures. He signed more than spoke. The leader nodded.

"What did you tell him?" Lewis asked.

"I told him we could give him a boat ride," Dorion said. "He can't have the boat, but we'll let him on board for a bit. I also told him that we had another present for him onboard."

"Present?" Lewis lifted his eyebrows.

Dorion grinned. "The whisky. These Sioux love firewater."

The Sioux were really happy with that. Lewis and Clark went on the boat with them, along with Dorion. They asked me to fetch the whisky, which I did. I joined them, and Dorion tried to talk with the leader. The Sioux passed the bottle around and took generous gulps. Half the bottle was gone within ten minutes. About ten minutes after that, we could see the effects. The leader's words slurred, and his warriors laughed uproariously. One of them accidentally fell out of the boat, and Dorion had to drag him back in.

In the end, they passed out. Clark was of the opinion that we should cut their throats and feed them to the catfish. Lewis, naturally, vetoed this plan. Instead, we let them sleep and went back to land to make camp. We might have had a bit much whisky, ourselves, and it wasn't long after the moon rose that we were ready for sleep.

The next day the Sioux were surprisingly unhungover, unlike the rest of us. They agreed to join us in the boats and sail upriver to their village. We made room for them onboard, and the leader, with Dorion's help, led the way. There he invited us into their lodge, which was actually a large teepee with a fire blazing within. Since we couldn't all go in, Lewis and Clark said the rest of us would draw straws. Dorion didn't have to, for obvious reasons. I did not get a short straw, so I don't know what happened in there.

I did take in the rest of the village. I'd never really had the chance to study the Sioux in broad daylight like this. Usually, we were doing the ceremonial thing and didn't have time for sightseeing. It was interesting to see them at work and play. Their children ran naked through the village. I think the idea of the game was to grab whoever is "it" and slap the back of his knee. When that happened, whoever did the slapping would then become "it." I scribbled some notes down in what remained of Chuck's journal. My chicken scratch probably just confused whoever read it later on, but I felt Chuck would have wanted me to do that.

Later that night—and we stayed with them a few days—the leader, who had a name I couldn't pronounce much less spell, invited us to one of their ceremonies. The next night we'd put on a military show for them with the .46 and, of course, drink more whisky. But that night we sat in a circle. Inside that circle was another circle of the women of the village. In that circle was a blazing fire that must have been ten feet high. They danced wildly around that fire, holding sticks aloft with some kind of material at the end. I thought it was some kind of cloth, and I mentioned it to Dorion.

"Nope," he said. "Those are scalps of their enemies."

I touched my own hair, and I felt a sudden chill come over me.

"Relax, Hi. None of 'em are white men. We're probably the first they've ever met. Aside from Frenchie trappers, maybe."

I saw one of the scalps was blond, but I decided not to point that out.

CHAPTER TWELVE

WE LEFT THE Lakota Sioux on September 29 and took back to the river. For the next two days nothing of interest happened. On the third day we saw a hastily assembled teepee with smoke drifting from the top. Nearby looked to be the stone foundation of a cabin. Stacks of logs rested nearby, waiting to be put together.

"A trapper?" Lewis asked.

Dorion shrugged. "I don't know."

"Perhaps we should check it out."

We beached ourselves, and Lewis and Dorion started toward the teepee.

"NO! NO! NONONONONONONONONONONONONO!!!!"

The scream startled all of us. Clark nearly jumped out of his boots, but he was quick on the draw. He glanced wildly around, looking for whomever he needed to shoot.

Then from the woods came a very hairy man. Except the top of the head. He looked very familiar to me.

"NO WHITE PEOPLE ALLOWED!" he screamed. "WHITE PEOPLE RUIN EVERYTHING!"

"Oh please, Lewis," Clark said. "Please let me shoot him."

Lewis looked like he briefly considered it, but he shook his head. "Holster your weapon, please."

"GET THE FUCK OUT OF THIS WILDERNESS!" The bald white man rushed into his teepee, and we heard him yelling obscenities. He finally emerged with his all too familiar carpet bag, bulging just like last time.

"Sir, we don't mean to intrude," Lewis said.

"SHUT THE FUCK UP! GO BACK TO FUCKVILLE WHERE YOU BELONG YOU FUCKING FUCKS!"

He ran behind a bush, behind which he pulled a canoe and an oar. He pushed into the river and paddled like a madman.

"We're only going to see him again," Clark said. "I can still hit him at this range."

Lewis shook his head.

The man shouted over his back, "EAT SHIT AND DIE MOTHERFUCKERS!"

He struck me as an older man, perhaps sixty, but he moved like he was in his prime. He disappeared over the horizon within minutes.

Clark turned to Lewis. "You should have let me shoot him."

Lewis said nothing to this. We moved on.

A few days later we saw an unbelievable sight. Up to that moment all we'd seen were small settlements. What we now saw was a veritable city. Huts and teepees as far as the eye could see. There was even a cabin with smoke drifting from the chimney. We later learned that more than two thousand—TWO THOUSAND!—people lived there.

We beached the boats and with backs loaded with supplies, we approached the city. Lo! and behold! A white man walked out of the cabin! He saw us immediately and approached swiftly, a smile on his face. A flurry of French rushed out of his mouth, confusing most of us. Dorion stepped forward, and *more* French confused the rest of us.

Dorion turned to us. "This man's name is Joseph Gravelines. He's been living here for a very long time."

"Does he speak English?" Lewis asked.

Dorion shook his head. "Very few fur traders from New France know it. But he knows the Arikara language very well."

"Arikara?" Lewis and Clark said in unison. "What does that mean?" Clark asked.

"That's the name of the natives who live here," Dorion said.

"I'd love it if he would show us around," Lewis said.

We didn't know it at the time, but Gravelines would be very important to us. We were mostly past the land and people Dorion knew, but Gravelines made up for it.

He gave us the tour, as the young people say these days. We went through the usual customs. Gift giving. The Jefferson coin. A demonstration of the .46. And, of course, whisky. We stayed there for a few days, and when we departed, Lewis offered a job to Gravelines.

He took it. Thank God.

CHAPTER THIRTEEN

IT HAPPENED AGAIN.

This time I have no idea why. I asked the offender, and he refused to say anything. I asked Lewis, and he said it was something despicable and not worth repeating. I got very much the same answer from everyone else (I didn't bother to ask Clark), so I gave up. All I know is something from Lewis's journal I read many years later, when it was published. He said Pvt. John Newman had "uttered repeated expressions of a highly criminal and mutinous nature." Still, he said nothing specific.

What I do know happened was that he was "chained and detained," a phrase of Clark's. It's not bad. I wouldn't have thought him capable of clever word play. I have no choice but to think he stole it from elsewhere.

After that detention Newman received seventy-five lashes. Oftentimes during this expedition there were men who looked away from this sort of thing. Lewis usually did. Not this time. Everyone watched, their excitement clear in their eyes. Clark seemed to find this punishment particularly delicious. He nearly drooled as he watched it.

Lewis then stripped Newman of his rank and cast him out of the Corps of Discovery. Since we were so deep into the wilderness, Newman followed us at a distance. He'd taken his lashes remarkably well. He had to be in utter pain at the time, but he kept pace with us. I'm sure he got what he deserved, but I can't say that he wasn't a tough son of a bitch.

Perhaps a week later we found a native dressing a dead deer. He'd gotten the organs out and set them aside, and now worked at removing the skin. He glanced toward us and dropped his knife, wiping his bloody hands on his pants. He wore no shirt.

By the time we were close enough to speak, he did so. Dorion stared back with a lack of understanding. Gravelines knew just what to say.

When he'd concluded, he turned to Dorion and spoke a lot of French. Dorion then turned to Lewis and Clark. "His name is Chief Big White of the Mandan tribe. Joey here told him about our expedition, and the chief has invited us to his village."

"Please tell him that we accept his invitation," Lewis said.

Soon we followed Chief Big White to one of the oddest settlements we've ever seen. There were no teepees or lodges. Instead, their dwellings were made of dried mud. I have no idea what they do when it rains. It never made sense to me, but that was the way of the Mandans and their companions, the Hidastas. We did all the usual things. I think I've mentioned them so many times I'm tired of it. From here on out, when a meeting occurs according to plan, just assume that we do the usual things.

But something different happened this time. Lewis and Clark stepped away from us. Not even York was invited to this private conference, and Clark required that York be by his side at every possible moment. The rest of us prepared luncheon and shared our food with curious natives.

When Lewis and Clark finished, they came back to us.

"Winter is approaching quickly," Lewis said. "Clark and I have decided that we will wait out the season here."

"I've already sent Gravelines to Chief Big White to ask permission," Clark said. I don't think he liked saying it. I suspect that he wanted to just take the village from the natives and hold it until spring. I can't prove it, but I got that feeling.

"So, starting tomorrow, we will build a fort here," Lewis said. "It will be called Ft. Mandan. It will be across the river there." He pointed. "So we don't interfere with the inner workings of the Mandan society."

Clark grunted.

"So tonight, we shall celebrate with our new friends. But not too much. Get some rest, as tomorrow will begin a months-long labor. Hopefully we'll be able to finish Ft. Mandan before it gets too cold and snowy."

And so, it was very hard work, but we met a lot of friends in this village. I think that more than made up for our backbreaking labor.

I thought I should mention, just for the sake of posterity, that John Newman sheltered with us during the time we built Ft. Mandan and for a while afterward. Still smarting from his wounds, he threw himself into the hard labor, mostly chopping down trees and forming the logs we would need for materiel. Everyone made fun of him. Never to his face, of course. You don't fuck with a man who can chop down fifty trees a day single-handedly. But behind his back, the rest of the corps was merciless. Not me. I had a suspicion that Newman was trying to atone for his crimes, whatever they were. When winter let up, Lewis ordered him back east, and he went. The way I heard it he lived in Missouri before becoming a trapper. The Yankton Sioux killed him, and that was that for our super man.

Back to our story. A couple of days into our labor, we were surprised by a man named Rene Jessaume. He told us he'd lived with the Mandans for years. And I mean *he* told us. His mother tongue is French, but he could speak English with very little accent. He also knew the Mandan language very well. Lewis hired him as a translator on the spot. Jessaume also helped with our labor. There were a few other French fur traders that came through, peddling their wares. Lewis bought a hefty pelt off of one, and throughout the winter it was rare to see him without it.

Barely a week passed before another trader arrived. His name was Baptiste Le Page. I don't think he was very good at his job, since he had nothing he wanted to trade. Instead, he asked Lewis for a job. Clark thought it would be a waste of time, but Lewis reminded him how many of the corps we'd lost, from poor Chuck Floyd to those they'd kicked out for sundry crimes and misdemeanors, most notably Newman. We were short and needed more men. That convinced Clark, so Le Page joined our crew.

And then we found yet another fur trader. We'd never met so many in one place in our entire journey. They all knew the Mandans and Hidatsas, but the idea of so many of them living in harmony with the natives surprised me. I'd never seen so many white faces in a native village before.

But this man was different. Not only did he live in harmony with the natives, he'd married two of them. His name was Toussaint Charbonneau, and he had the most well-groomed set of mustaches I've ever seen with just a sliver of a beard hanging down his chin. I'd never seen anything like that before. These days, it's more in style. I suppose it all began with him, though I can't be too sure.

Both of his wives were Shoshone. One, Otter Woman, doesn't figure into this narrative much. It's the other wife that stands out. I could make the argument that she is the greatest known native woman in our history. Her name was Sacagawea.

I didn't learn until much later that the marriage was not exactly consensual. She'd been captured by the Hidatsas when she was twelve, and a year later she was sold to Charbonneau. By the time we met her, she must have let it go. She seemed pretty happy. She was also very pregnant. She looked like she could pop at any minute. But we'll get back to her in a bit.

There isn't much of note for the next month. There is just one thing that happened, and it was me who did it. I'd been taking a break from our labors when I heard screams from the other side of the river. I went to our supplies and picked up a scope. I extended it and peered through to see what was going on.

A bear rampaged through the Mandans' village. Its target seemed to be a group of children who ran desperately toward the river, hoping to escape the beast. I dropped the scope and went for the .46. By now I'd had enough practice to be considered a crack shot. I took careful aim because the children were between me and the bear. I held my breath, let my hands grow steady. I let the breath out as I pulled the trigger. The gun roared, and a split second later the bear fell flat on its face and skidded on the ground.

"Hot damn! That was an excellent shot, Hi."

I turned and saw Lewis behind me. I had no idea he'd been back there, watching. Clark stood next to him, but he had no praise for me. He had no praise for anyone except maybe himself.

"Let's get over there," Lewis said.

We both went to a boat with Clark shuffling reluctantly behind us. York went with us, too, as we rowed across the river to the dead bear. Already the natives had gathered around it, awed by such a quick death for a large and monstrous beast. Jessaume was already there, and he whistled, impressed.

"Who took that shot?" he asked.

"It was Hi," Lewis said. He clapped me on the back.

"That was some fine shooting," Jessaume said. "You shot it through the eye and directly into the brain. I've never seen someone do that before."

I felt my cheeks redden. No one, not even Pa, had ever praised me in such a manner.

Charbonneau arrived, and we went through the whole thing again. He said, "I'll skin it. The fur is yours, Hi. You earned it. As for the rest of the beast..."

"I think we will eat very fine this day," Lewis said.

And dine we did. When Charbonneau had my bear pelt ready, I was grateful. Winter's smoky breath already chilled our necks. I still have that pelt today. I took great pride in it.

Nothing else of note happened, and on December 24 we finished Ft. Mandan and moved in directly. I wound up with some nice quarters. Even better than the farm I grew up on. Better than when I lived in La Charrette, and that one came with an occasional whore.

It got drafty, but I had my bear pelt, and that kept me very warm for the months to come.

CHAPTER FOURTEEN

WE'D DONE SO much celebrating over the course of the year we'd been on this expedition, but the biggest was probably our New Year's soiree. We mostly kept to ourselves, but some of the fur traders were there, as were a select few natives, among them Chief Big White. Usually, the music we enjoyed in the past belonged to the natives, but this night we had our own music. Field had a fiddle, which he played very well. All the other music we enjoyed that day had that fiddle at the center. There was dancing and singing and we got deep into the whisky. Very few of us remembered that night. How aggravating it must have been for those on guard! When morning came, we replaced them with sentries harboring thick and vicious hangovers.

After that everything went back to normal. Nothing of note really happened during that time. Some of the men tried to buy wives from the Mandans, but Lewis forbade it. So did Clark, but not for the same reason. Lewis didn't want things to get complicated. The expedition was rough enough as it was. Clark, on the other hand, became furious at the idea that white men might have children with "the savages." No surprise there.

But the next month passed very uneventfully. And then February came, and with it another punishment meted out.

It happened on the ninth. One of our men, Thomas Howard, accidentally got locked out of the fort. In my opinion, overall, he was not a smart man. He was good at fixing things. A great laborer. He even made gimcracks for the Mandan children in his spare time. But a great thinker he was not. So, upon learning he could not gain access to the fort, he did what any idiot would have done: he scaled the wall. One of the Mandans watched him do it and immediately followed his example. Upon learning this Lewis was mortified.

Clark, naturally, was enraged.

For once their feelings were for the same reason. While the Mandans weren't technically our enemy, it would be bad form to show them how easy it would be to get into our fort on the off-chance that they might decide to raid us, which was a constant concern for Clark.

This time Lewis advocated strongly for punishment. The trial did not last long, as it was a foregone conclusion that Howard was guilty. Lewis sentenced him to fifty lashes for "setting a pernicious example to the savages." He didn't usually call them savages. I thought Clark might have been wearing off on him. Regardless, Lewis decided to mete out the fifty lashes himself. It was ugly, but it was the final time anyone would be whipped during our expedition. Thankfully.

Just a few days after this, Lewis, Clark, York, Joe Field and myself were on the other side of the river among the Mandans. We were looking for trade, but we didn't get the chance. A frantic Charbonneau rushed through the village screaming for a midwife. We all knew what was happening. Lewis, having had some experience, went to him to offer his aid.

We all went to his cabin. There we found Sacagawea on the floor, her knees pointed up, her legs wide open. A puddle of her water spread from between those legs. She screamed and breathed heavily. Lewis got into position, just as he had months ago, and he gave her instructions on what to do. Charbonneau translated, as she didn't speak much English.

It wasn't an easy birth, but Lewis finally pulled a boy out of her. I know this is difficult to believe, but the straw that broke the camel's back was part of a rattlesnake's rattler. Jessaume just happened by and heard the screams. He offered Lewis the rattle, and he took it apart and mixed it with water like a witch doctor. To this day I don't know how that worked, but after that the boy slid right out.

Charbonneau named his son Jean Baptiste, and the little one would soon join us on our expedition with his mother and father.

A quick word about the young lad. Despite being the offspring of a so-called "savage," Clark actually liked the kid. I can't explain why, just as much as I can't explain why he nicknamed Jean Baptiste "Pompey." Regardless, after we eventually returned east Clark made sure he received an excellent education, and from there he became a worldwide adventurer and spoke four languages very well. I don't know what Africa is like, but Pompey certainly found out for himself. He became a very famous man of the world to the point where I tell my fellow elders that I was there when he was born. None of them believe me.

After that, Clark doted on the boy whenever he was free from his duties. We all waited out the rest of the winter. Sometimes things got tough, and we got hungry. We ran out of food after a while and had to eat some of our horses to survive. Horse is too stringy to be a good meal, but it did, indeed, keep us alive. Alive long enough that when game finally wandered toward the river when it was no longer frozen, we were able to eat and eat well.

The cold let up, and the snow left us, but we waited just in case it was a false alarm. When we were certain that spring had joined us for real, we made plans to leave the fort behind.

Lewis and Clark now regretted letting us eat some of the horses, since we were now ridiculously short of them. We needed more. Charbonneau said that if we continued our path, we would eventually reach Shoshone territory, where we would be able to trade for more horses. The problem was, they weren't a very friendly people. However, if we brought Sacagawea, a native Shoshone, with us as a translator, they would most likely do business with us. Lewis and Clark agreed to take Charbonneau and Sacagawea (and little Pompey) with us.

CHAPTER FIFTEEN

JOE FIELD CAME rushing back to us after being gone for a day. "Sirs! I just saw something you won't ever believe!"

We'd heard that line from him so many times that we were getting bored of it. The only thing is, he was rarely wrong.

When Lewis asked him for clarification Field didn't explain. "You just have to see it for yourself."

We rode—or, at least, those of us with horses rode—nearly five miles when we saw a village up ahead. There was a great big gate and a fence that ran around it. It was rickety and could have been knocked over by an ant's fart, so it clearly was not meant for defense purposes. There was a sign above the gate, and it bore one word and one word only.

CROATOAN.

I'd never seen Lewis shocked in my whole life, and he cursed very rarely. But when he saw that sign, his jaw dropped. "Holy motherfucking shit."

Clark, who loved to curse with great gusto, looked at him. "Watch your language, asshole."

They looked at each other seriously for a moment, and then they broke into an uncontrollable case of the giggles. It spread quickly through the expedition, and even I had difficulty breathing through my laughter. Sgt. Gass fell off his horse, he was laughing so hard. Those without horses grasped their bellies and fell to their knees. I'm sure they could have heard our laughter in merry olde England. Even Sacagawea laughed, and she had no idea why. It caused Pompey to give out gurgly baby noises.

When Lewis could finally hold a straight face, he let out a tremendous breath. "I think we finally have an answer to one of America's greatest mysteries."

On that note we approached the village. As we drew closer, we noticed something very interesting. There were a lot of white faces here. A lot of red faces, too. And a lot of faces that looked mixed. All of them dressed like natives. I glanced at Clark, just to gauge his expression, but he had none to offer.

When they saw us, they ran and hid away, or so we thought. A very large woman with a headdress of feathers came forward to greet us.

"Hello, travelers," she said. In English!

"Hello," Lewis said. He introduced himself and Clark, and nodded to the rest of us as "our corps." "And who might you be?"

"My name is Josephine Dare," she said. "Pleased to make your acquaintance."

Lewis and Clark exchanged a glance. Lewis said, "Any relation to Virginia Dare, by any chance?"

"She was my I-don't-know-how-many-greats grandmother. Among the first to be born in the New World." She beamed with pride, like she'd had something to do with it.

More of the villagers wandered closer, and I could hear them whispering to each other. Some of it was in English, and some in another language I couldn't understand. I looked to our translators to see if they got any of it. Not one of them did.

"Please, welcome to our village," Josephine said. "Croatoan is free to one and all."

"Free?" Lewis asked.

"That's right. Here we share all possessions, all food. And we do not allow slavery here."

I glared at Clark for a moment, but he didn't seem to notice. He turned to York. "You are to remain outside of this village."

York grimaced like he might have accidentally swallowed a booger. "Yes, master."

I thought about mentioning that she'd said "slavery" and not "slaves," but I don't know what good that would have done. It might even have done harm for York.

Lewis and Clark led the expedition into the village. I hung back for a moment, pretending to go over my pack horse. When they were out of earshot, I turned to York. "You gonna be good out here?"

York glanced at the people we'd just met, and an odd look came across his face. I had no idea what it meant. It looked almost fearful, but it might have been revulsion. I don't know.

"I'll be fine," York said.

I didn't do this for just anybody in our group, but I felt bad that York had to sit this one out. Besides I liked York more than most in that corps. I offered him a bottle of my private whisky stock. He smiled but declined.

"You need any help, call out for me," I said.

He nodded, and I led my horses into the village.

At this point the introductions were being made. I caught up and got in line with the rest. Lewis was doing the talking, and Clark, now realizing the different colored faces, sat on his horse scowling. And then Lewis introduced me as Hi Ziege.

"Interesting," Josephine said. "An unusual name, I think."

"Not so much back home, ma'am," I said.

"German?" she asked.

"Yes ma'am."

"We actually have a man in this village with the last name of Ziege. Could he possibly be of relation to you?"

"No telling, ma'am. Us Zieges get around." That's the truth. Pa used to talk about his brothers and their Pa. They came from overseas together, but their Pa died when a barrel of whisky fell on him from an upper deck, and one of his brothers died because he thought the ocean was good drinking water. There were ten brothers that survived and spread out through this land. I didn't know any of them. I met one later, long after the expedition was over. He advised me that Pa was always kind of crazy. But he insisted that the stories about him and goats were absolutely true. Apparently, I have brothers overseas, and all of them, he said, looked kind of like me, since I looked a lot like Pa.

Josephine turned around and cupped her hands to her mouth. "Cephus! Get over here! I got someone you might want to meet!"

A tall figure with a woolen head wandered out from behind a cabin, and I'll be damned if he didn't have the Ziege face. Or, at least, what was left of it. And he only had one hand!

"Brother Cephus!" I shouted.

"Brother?" Cephus asked.

I explained to him that I knew about him through Pa, about how he explained the incident with the bear trap. When I said that, he grinned, showing off a tangle of teeth just like mine.

"Hot damn! Brother Hieronymus!" He opened his arms, and we hugged, clapping each other on the back.

"How'd you know my name? You left before I was born."

"You called yourself Hi. That was Pa's middle name."

That struck me as odd. Now, as an old man, I understand how stupid I'd been. I'd thought that Pa's name was Pa Ziege. It never occurred to me that he had a real name.

Lewis smiled. "Brothers reunited in the wilderness! I think this calls for a celebration!"

And it was a blow out. A real blow out. We all built a campfire that blazed to the heavens, and we danced and sang and drank. Oh, we drank. I remember Jacques back in La Charrette, and how he once tried to drunkenly jump in the river to swim to England for vengeance. That night in Croatoan, I found myself so drunk that I thought maybe he could have made it.

Every once in a while, I looked back to the gate, to where York had made camp. He seemed to be doing fine by himself. The next day he thanked me for bringing him some meat fresh off the spit, but I had no recollection of doing that.

We all nearly drank ourselves into an early grave, and half of us were passed out in various positions. Several of our men ended up in cabins with the ladies of Croatoan. That's another thing that Josephine explained to us. They weren't mango...monogamis. I forget the word. They shared lovers, is what I mean to say. They could fuck whomever they wanted to. I have to say, I kinda like that idea. It would solve a lot of our problems.

I don't know when I passed out, but when I woke up with a pounding headache and a queasy feeling in my guts, I saw that my shirt was open, and my pants were down to my boots. My dick lay like a club on my leg nearly to the knee. I grabbed up my pants just in case there were ladies present.

And that's when I noticed something strange. Almost everyone was gone. The buildings were still there, but the only people left were members of the corps. Where did everyone else go?

I had to take a piss, so I went up to a wall and relieved myself. When I did so, the stream broke up and went in odd directions like it usually did when I had sex. Who did I fuck last night?

I shook off and tucked myself away. By then others were waking up, probably feeling very much like me. Clark stumbled like it was his first time walking. He nearly fell and hit his head on a tree. Lewis, who had imbibed more than he usually did, had to brace himself against a fence in order to stand. The worst of us, Gass, crawled on hands and knees until he could sit with a cabin at his back.

"Where did everyone go?" Joe Field asked.

"You all finally awake?"

I turned to see York approaching us from the gate. He no longer had a problem with being denied access to this place. I glanced to Clark to see what he thought, but he was still trying to regain some semblance of balance.

"Did you see where everyone went?" I asked.

"They disappeared," York said.

"We know that," Clark muttered. "Where'd they go?"

"No, they literally disappeared. I'm surprised that you're so surprised."

"What do you mean?"

York looked around, and it seemed like he was reluctant to say something. "You all were partying with ghosts last night."

"Don't be fucking ridiculous!" Clark roared. He flinched, unprepared to mete out such anger during such a hangover.

"What about my brother?" I asked. "Where did he go?"

"He was dead, too," York said.

"That's impossible," Lewis said. But there seemed to be some doubt in his voice.

"Captains!" Field shouted. "Over here!"

We followed the sound of his voice to the back of the village, and there we saw row after row of white crosses sticking out of the ground, all bearing names. Field stood in front of one that had Josephine Dare's name on it. Pale as a ghost, he pointed a trembling finger. He might have been trembling from fear or the hangover, I don't know.

I searched among the graves, seeking out my brother's, but he wasn't there. I tried to remember which cabin was his, and I left the others behind to find it. The door hung open, and I stepped into the darkness inside. It stank like a goat's pen, and it reminded me of home. I wondered how Jeb was doing, if the farm was still going well. I wondered if he ever found the goat of his dreams, and if he had, did they have a family? I know the answer to that now, but then I was stuck in the past. A smell will do that to you.

I threw open the shutters of a window to let some light in, and I saw a bed with a person-sized lump under it.

"Cephus?" I asked.

It didn't stir.

I peeled the blanket back to see my brother, dead by many, many years. There wasn't much skin left, but the teeth were undeniable. I again found myself in a wondering place. Did my brother find this place and live among them? Had they been alive at the time? I think what happened was, he left us before I was born and took to the wilderness. He found this place, and they were all still alive. Maybe some sickness came along and killed everyone. I think he dug those graves and buried those people. But he was the last to die, and there was no one left to bury him.

I sensed a change in the light, and I turned to see a figure standing in the door, blocking out the sun. York.

"That your brother?" he asked.

I nodded.

"We'd best put him with the others, then."

He helped me roll Cephus up into a bundle and carry him out to the cemetery. We both dug the grave and filled it in, while Lewis found wood for a cross. I wrote Cephus's name on it and planted it. I don't know how religious he might have been, so I thought it might be good to say a few words. I fumbled through it from memory. Then we gathered our things to move on.

"Let's put this godforsaken place behind us," Clark said.

About a week later, we came to another river and set up camp. Field came back from ahead with a set of giant horns. He described something he called a big horn sheep, which sounded pretty crazy. Most of us wouldn't have believed him if he hadn't come back with those horns. We added them to our collection while Lewis scouted out the area, thinking a fort could be built here in the future. I think they did, eventually, build a fort there. The name escapes my mind, though. It's in modern day Montana Territory.

Ever onward. We traveled mostly by boat, so when a storm rushed up and kicked us in the ass, one of boats capsized. It contained a lot of our collection so far, including several journals, one of them Chuck's mysterious journal, the one he was writing a translation in. We were all busy fighting the current, so we almost didn't notice.

Sacagawea dove in and single-handedly rescued almost all of it. I don't rightly know what we lost. I wasn't in charge of inventory. But she managed to save Chuck's surviving journal, the one that eventually got published. I know that much.

When the storm calmed, I'll be goddammed if Clark didn't praise her for her quick thinking. That's right. You read that right. *Clark.*

Not too long after that came another bear fight. We were moving on land by then, and the biggest fucking bear we've ever seen came rushing out of the trees at us. It was big as God and just as furious.

The .46 wasn't meant for up close work, so we had to rely on the guns at our hips. Everyone fired at the thing, and it didn't seem to do any harm. Lewis and I, at the same time, fired. Each of our minie balls found an eye, and the bear dropped dead instantly. I looked over at Lewis, and he grinned. I nodded back and reloaded, just in case this crazy bastard had a brother.

We ate pretty good the next few days. The fur traders once more skinned the bear and worked on its pelt. There was enough to make blankets for ten men, but Lewis and Clark got the biggest ones.

Shortly after that, we reached one of the strangest sights I've ever seen. Stranger than the weird man who keeps telling us to go to Fuckville. Or was he saying we were from Fuckville? I don't rightly know. But it was not as strange as the literal ghost town of Croatoan.

It looked like a river of milk. Sacagawea, having been from these parts, already knew about it. She said it was "a river which scolds all others." It came to be known as Milk River, named such by Lewis himself. He wrote about it in his journal, which was not one of the ones recently water damaged, so it was pretty clear for historians to read.

As always, we moved on.

CHAPTER SIXTEEN

AND THEN WE fucked up.

We came to a fork in the river. So far, we'd been using the Missouri River as a guide, more or less, but this was a new one on us. The fur traders had never been this far out, so they had no idea what to do. Not even Sacagawea knew, and she used to live around here. Then again, it had been a while since she was kidnapped as a child. I guess she had other things on her mind back then.

Now that the river forked, we didn't know which way to go. Lewis and Clark were adamant about sticking to the Missouri, but we didn't know which way the Missouri went, north or south?

We set up camp here. Clark decided to call it Camp Deposit, since he planned on caching some supplies here. I didn't understand the concept at the time. Why leave supplies we might need behind? On the way back I figured it out. It was a backup plan in case we got fucked in the ass by nature again. The corps dug a hole and put all sorts of things in there, from smithing tools to the bear pelts from our recent kill. They then filled the hole. They also hid the boat that carried all that stuff just off the rivers. Pryor had a bad shoulder that popped out on occasion. It happened here, and he screamed bloody murder before he was able to snap it back in place. It still hurt, so he managed to sit out the rest of the job.

After that everyone started arguing about which way to go. I stayed out of it. I had no idea, and I think if you don't have anything to say, just don't say anything. I had a sneaking suspicion it was the north fork, because we tended toward northwest, but what the hell did I know?

Finally, they decided to send scouts down each branch. Sgt. Gass was assigned to the south, and he chose to take with him LePage and Field. Sgt. Pryor was assigned to the north, and he chose to take with him Dorion and me. We set off right away, and I have no idea what happened with Gass's team. All I know is that when we came back, we'd both reached the same conclusion: who the fuck knows?

So, we argued more. The one thing that we knew for certain, thanks to Sacagawea and Charbonneau, was that the Missouri River has a great waterfall somewhere around here. If we could confirm which direction that waterfall was, we'd know which fork to take.

Almost all of us thought it was the north fork, but Lewis and Clark and a smattering of others had it into their heads that it was the south fork. I kept out of it, but I still couldn't figure out why they would think the falls were to the south. It seemed obvious to me that they would be to the north. But I didn't know anything. I let the smarter men do the thinking.

This didn't happen often on our journey, but the minority won out the argument, probably because both of our leaders were in said minority. So, we went down the south fork for a while. We rested on land every evening, but while we still had light left in the sky, Lewis took a crew of men with him to scout ahead. Every night, just as the sun disappeared over the horizon, they would return with no new information.

I should mention at this time that Joe Field had a brother with us on the expedition. Reubin Field was a lot like his brother, but there was a bit of an edge to him that Joe lacked. That edge made him a bit meaner. Whenever Lewis went on his evening jaunts, he almost always took both brothers with him. Once I got a bit curious and thought maybe I should go, too, but I remembered I'd see whatever they saw the next day, anyway. So I got some sleep in.

Shit. That's going to complicate things some. I guess I'll have to refer to them by their first names now, just to differentiate. It's a little funny. I saw Reubin in St. Louis not too long after the expedition was over. This was about the time that Lewis and Clark's journals were published, and he was irritated because neither of them got his and his brother's last name right. It's Field, not Fields. I tried not to laugh, but it is kind of funny.

One day, after Lewis and his team disembarked on their scouting mission, Joe Field came rushing back to camp. All of us thought they'd run into trouble and needed immediate assistance. We all loaded up our horses in anticipation of what would undoubtedly be violence.

Instead, he handed a note to Clark. It took Clark a moment to read it, as he barely knows how to read, but then a smile broke out on his face. He turned to the rest of us. "Lewis found the falls!"

Well, I'll be damned. Good thing I didn't shoot my mouth off back when we were at the fork. A lot of us glanced to each other, feeling very stupid.

So, we celebrated that night. We got shitfaced in no time at all. When Lewis and the rest made it back to us, we were well into our cups. They had to fight to catch up. But here's the thing none of us thought about that night. We had to find some way around the falls, and that would mean a lot of physical labor.

When we woke up the next morning we were not fit for any labor, much less physical. We dragged our carcasses onto the boats and made our way forward, bitching to each other about the hell we were about to encounter.

Lewis, usually the clearest thinker of us, called for lunch, and we took to the land, much refreshed after getting some food down our guts. He wasn't hungover like the rest of us, so he went for a walk to stretch his legs. When he came back, it was by the river instead of the land. He was so exhausted from swimming that we had to drag him back to the grass.

"What happened?" Clark asked.

It took Lewis a moment to catch his breath. Then: "A fucking bear. That's what happened." Apparently, he'd shot a bison, thinking it would make a good dinner, but it didn't die right away. While he waited a bear—one of the giant kind that live around this area—came out of nowhere and wound up chasing him to the river. When he jumped in, he swam for all he was worth, and the bear gave up, probably because the bison was right there. Why go for a carrot when the steak is closer?

We finally made it to the falls, and though we weren't suffering as badly as earlier, we were still in a rotten mood. We went to land and made camp while the Field brothers went scouting for ways we could get around the falls.

A word about the falls. They are technically called the Great Falls of the Missouri River. It got named that because that's the way Lewis wrote it in his journal. When he used the word "great," he was not fucking around. We had to cart everything down an entire mountain in order to get around the falls. It took us days, and even the most optimistic of us hated every second of it.

That wasn't the only thing we did in that time. Several projects formed, which didn't help us with the grunt work. While most of us toiled getting entire boats down a mountain, someone came up with an insane plot to build an iron ship. A fucking iron ship. One that, in the end, we couldn't even use because it sank when finished. A fucking iron ship!

Lewis worked on building another of his caches while Clark surveyed the land. He found something that we now call the Giant Springs. It would have been more helpful if they worked with the rest of us, but when I saw the Giant Springs, I actually thought it was beautiful. Good call on that one, Clark.

But the iron boat thing fucked us. We had to come up with something else. By then we'd gotten everything down to the bottom of the falls. We spent a few days to build two new canoes. Thankfully I knew nothing about building canoes, so I didn't have to take part in that. Many of us not involved took to wandering around. Never alone, though. Lewis's story of the bear was all too fresh in our minds. I usually tagged along with the Field brothers.

One day, shortly before we would set forth again, I was very glad I had the Field brothers with me. We discovered something very strange, and if I'd seen it alone, no one else would have believed me.

Reubin had to take a shit, so Joe and I kept ourselves busy busting each other's balls. We were laughing and having a good time, and Joe tried to bullshit me over this whore he was with once who had three tits. All things considered I kind of believe him now. After that expedition and all the crazy shit we'd all seen, especially Al and the Croatoan village and the cannibals I haven't gotten to yet, why not a three-tittied woman?

Reubin came rushing up to us, barely holding his pants up, and judging by the stink, I didn't think he'd had the chance to wipe. He looked scared and pale, and he kept looking over his shoulder.

"What happened?" Joe asked.

"That!" Reubin said. He fell in with us and turned around, pointing.

A creature, humanoid in shape, rose up before us maybe seven feet tall. He—and it was a he judging by the giant hairy cock hanging between his legs—was covered in thick fur from head to toe except his face, very much like a simian. He didn't have a nose, but had two thin slit nostrils. His eyes were definitely human, with the color part surrounded by a bunch of white with red veins in it.

"Look at that sumbitch!" Reubin said. "Look at 'is feet!"

We looked, and they were, indeed, huge. Being tall, I got big feet to match the rest of me. But I probably could have fit both my feet in this creature's footprint and still have room left over.

"It's a Bigfoot," Joe said. Like he'd seen one of them before. Just as calm as can be.

"What?" I said.

"You heard me."

Well, I had. But I didn't mean it like that. I wanted clarification.

"You know what this is?" Reubin asked.

Joe shrugged. "Not really. But he don't seem angry with us. And those are some pretty big feet."

The thing looked at us curiously, kind of like when you stop petting a dog, and it looks at you wondering if you're really gonna stop. Its hands, much like its feet, were huge, and they looked like they could crush a chuckwagon in one go. I had my hand on the butt of my pistol, just in case. I expected I wouldn't need it, though. Neither Field brother did the same, so I figured one of us should.

The Bigfoot scratched his head, now looking more like a student trying to solve a math problem, and then he smiled at us. Big ol' teeth that looked a lot like ours. Well, more like Joe's. He had good teeth. Natural, too.

The Bigfoot then turned around and gestured to us to follow. He went deeper into the woods, and we passed by where Reubin had done his business. He took the moment to clean himself with some leaves and fell behind a bit, but Joe and I were grateful for the gesture. We went on for about an hour before we came to a village of Bigfoots. Or are they Bigfeet? I don't rightly know. We'll go with Bigfoots. They were all over the place. We even saw the women, tits out and all. Not one of them was put out by it, any. Their kids, just barely shorter than me, ran around like children would. The guy who invited us brought us to a giant tree with a hollow in it. It was fairly spacious in there, and I think it was his home. Or rather, his family's home. He had a wife and two kids. We sat around, and they shared some fruit with us. Really friendly folks.

People these days don't believe me when I tell them about this. Now that we're so widespread across this country they think they're so smart when they say that they've never seen a Bigfoot, so they can't exist. Sorry. I don't know what to tell you. I just know what I saw with my eyes. Joe came to a bad end not long after the expedition, but I've talked about this a few times whenever I run into Reubin. He gets the same response so much he stopped telling the story. Not me, though. I guess I'm just stubborn.

We tried to learn their language, but none of us had much of a brain. I wished one of the fur traders were with us. If anyone could learn it, they would. They picked up languages like one picks up sticks for a fire. Then again, maybe the traders would have wanted to give our new friends a full-body scalping, so maybe not such a good idea. We managed to get by with using our hands to talk. We could more or less understand them.

From what we could tell, they offered us a place to stay the night, but we knew we had to get back to the expedition. We did our best to explain ourselves, and we must have done a good job because they smiled at us, and the Bigfoot who brought us here walked us out to where we'd been.

We reached camp just as the last of the light disappeared from the sky. Before we got all the way back, we agreed that we wouldn't talk about what we'd just done. I was kind of reluctant because that was the whole purpose of the expedition. Joe and Reubin rightly figured that if not Lewis, then definitely Clark, would want us to bring them to the Bigfoot village to obtain a sample to send back to Tommy Jeff, as Clark sometimes called the president.

That convinced me. At least until we reached our destination. In that time, I confessed it to Charbonneau, who had heard of such things but had never actually seen one. It was more or less a legend among the French fur traders. He also asked, not too subtly, if I could show him where they lived. "No reason," he said. "Just curious."

I told him I'd never be able to find it again, which was at least half true. He seemed annoyed, but he let it go.

Not too long after, we left the falls and continued on our way. We went through what would be called Gates of the Mountains, and it sure was a beautiful sight. That and the Great Falls and the Giant Springs. I miss those most. If I weren't such an old man, I'd venture out there to see them again before I die, which will probably happen soon. It would be easier now that the trail has been blazed, but still. Old is old, and that's all there is to it.

Then we got to Three Forks. Lewis and Clark immediately panicked, much like they had when we had to figure out which fork was the Missouri River. Sacagawea assured us that this was supposed to be here, and it was still technically the Missouri River. All forks eventually came back together. In fact, this was where she'd been kidnapped before she'd been sold to Charbonneau.

We set up camp, and this time Clark scouted ahead to figure out which fork was the best to take. When he failed to report back, Lewis got aggravated and went after him. I don't know what that meeting was like, so I can't say anything about it. All I know is that they both came back together, and we took the north fork.

They named it after Tommy Jeff. I don't even think they were kidding when they said that.

A few days later it was Clark's thirty-fifth birthday. We set up camp to celebrate, but this time we'd learned our lesson from the Great Falls and didn't wake up the next day quite so hungover.

Maybe two weeks later we saw the first of the Shoshone. He was the first native we'd seen since Ft. Mandan. We would have missed him if Sacagawea hadn't pointed him out. Lewis saw him and tried to approach, but the man must not have wanted to talk. He retreated pretty quickly. Sacagawea said a few things, and it sounded angry, but Charbonneau decided he didn't want to translate that one.

We set up camp early, but Lewis couldn't sit still. He had to find that Shoshone man. While the rest of us settled in he scouted ahead. We didn't see him for a few days, and Clark made the call to stay here and wait. But during the third day he decided to send out a few scouts.

Before they could head out Lewis came back with the Shoshone man. His name was Cameahwait. It turned out that he wasn't just a Shoshone chief, he was also Sacagawea's brother. Small world.

It turns out that Lewis did something historical while he was gone and before he caught up to Cameahwait. He crossed something called the Continental Divide and was the first white man to do it. I don't know what any of that means, but I thought mentioning it in my book might make me look a bit smarter.

Damn, we were all so historical, weren't we?

We decided to call our spot Camp Fortune and stayed for a few days. We'd stay there while a deal was negotiated with the Shoshone tribe, who lived not too far away.

Maybe a couple of days later Lewis and Clark, with Sacagawea and her sister-in-law (if that's the right term, or maybe they were sisters, I don't recall), set out with Cameahwait, York, Joe Field, Charbonneau, Dorion and myself to the village. It was a nice place. Friendly people. A lot of people were happy with Sacagawea's return. And Charbonneau's other wife, Otter Woman. Not much gets said about her. I think that's because Sacagawea overshadowed her almost all of the time. They had a celebration, and most of our group celebrated with them and introduced them to whisky. They introduced Joe to...I don't know what, but it made him lay on the ground and stare up at the sky and say, "Wow," a lot. He seemed to like it.

Now that I think on it, there were a lot of people there who came to a bad end regarding our journey. Cameahwait certainly did. Too bad. I liked him. Hell, even Clark liked him. In his journal he called Cameahwait "a man of Influence Sence & easey & reserved manners, appears to possess a great deel of Cincerity." I know I got bad grammar, but Clark really had his way with words.

I watched Cameahwait play with Pompey, the little nephew he never knew he had. I had a funny feeling at the moment. Even so far from our civilization, another completely different civilization had been created, and it acted a lot like our own. It never ceases to amaze me that both civilizations usually hate each other for what, I believe, is essentially nothing.

While we were all going mad with drink and cheer, Lewis and a few of the others were in serious talks with the Shoshone. I dropped by every once in a while. So did York, who occasionally brought a bottle of whisky to them, ordered by Clark, naturally. I heard snippets here and there. One of the big ones I heard was about how our path ahead was nearly impassible. It gave me pause, and I remembered dealing with the Great Falls. Holy fuck, how could this get any worse? The way Cameahwait told it, we wouldn't be able to use the Missouri River to get through. There would be long stretches of mountains. I thought about us carrying those boats for miles, and I had to console myself with some of my private whisky stock.

I stumbled back once to see how things were going. Lewis wanted forty horses, and I thought that would probably lighten our load. Plus, the Shoshone had horses. Lots of them. Hundreds. They could afford to trade with us.

They wanted a lot in return. Maybe too much. They were hungry, and the reason we'd run into Cameahwait in the first place was because he was scouting for a big buffalo hunt. But then, if we were going into impassible territory, we knew we'd need our own food supply. It was plain that the Shoshone had been eating their own horses at this point. Not the best of cuisine. To be avoided when possible. Hell, we did the same thing at Ft. Mandan. That's why we were in this need of horses so badly in the first place.

They also wanted guns. Every once in a while, they'd find a French fur trader. They got a few rifles from them when they could. They traded more with the Spanish, but they refused to trade firearms. Lewis explained why we couldn't do that, either, and he did a good job of it. Since I'm looking at the journals, here's something he said in his: "If we had guns, we could live in the country of the buffaloe and eat as our enimies do, and not be compelled to hide ourselves in these mountains and live on roots and berries as the bear do." Lewis at least understood people and the things they'd respond to. Clark, on the other hand, just wanted to be a dick about it and say no.

Lewis even went the extra mile. He promised that his countrymen would eventually come back to Shoshone territory, and they "would come to them with a number of guns and every other article necessary to their defence and comfort."

I think that sealed the deal. The last time I wandered close they made their agreement. In exchange for twenty-nine horses, the Shoshone would get clothes, powder, balls and a pistol. Lewis and Clark also hired Old Toby as part of the deal.

A word about Old Toby. He was hired because he knew the best way through what would be known as the Bitterroot Mountains, and he would be our guide for this stretch. His real name was something I can't pronounce much less spell. It meant Swooping Eagle. So, I have no idea why we started calling him Old Toby, aside from the fact that he was an old man. But Toby? This baffled me for years, but when I found out from someone's journal—I forget which, and I don't want to look it up in a ridiculously high pile of journals—that it was an abbreviation of a bigger nickname. Again, I could look up the spelling of that one, but I don't have much time left in this world. What it meant was "furnished white white-man brains." What in the fuck that means? I don't know. I think someone was making fun of him. He was kind of a dick, so I'm okay with that.

I heard that he died of typhoid a few years ago. Couldn't have happened to a better man.

That's unfair. He did help us get through the Bitterroots. He may have been a gruff individual, and when he was around things sometimes went missing. When he left us, he did it by night with a couple of our horses. But we were alive when he left us, and I suppose that's all that counts.

Anyway, we all agreed, and that's when the Shoshone brought out their peace pipe. I just looked at it in Lewis's journal. He had a decent ability with drawing, but it doesn't do the real thing justice. This thing was big, and there was a lot packed inside it. I think we all thought it was tobacco, and maybe it was, but when the Shoshone smoked it, they held the smoke in their chests for a while before blowing it out. So that's what we did. York and I happened to be there at the same time, so they all invited us to join them. When the peace pipe came to me, I sucked in the smoke, and it had an odd odor. Fir trees mixed with skunk, maybe. The smoke tasted odd, too, and when I blew it out, I felt a bit lightheaded. And then I became very relaxed.

And then I passed it on to York. I spoke with him a few times after, and we agreed there was something different about that tobacco. He'd felt the same effect.

Whatever it was, it clashed with the whisky I'd already had, and I passed out early. The party continued without me.

The next day was Lewis's thirty-first birthday. We surprisingly didn't celebrate it. I knew it only because I overheard Clark talking about it to York. I read later in Lewis's journal that he called himself lazy and made a promise to himself that he would help people for the rest of his life.

I don't know why he wrote this. It's insane. I never knew someone with more energy, more curiosity, more generosity, than Meriwether Lewis. I remembered a few frustrated moments he had, but he never lacked for the things he wanted of himself.

CHAPTER SEVENTEEN

WE RESUMED OUR journey after that birthday. Lewis didn't even mention it to us. He seemed content with the idea that we were moving on. A few days later we all crossed that Continental Divide. I looked it up and found out why it was so historical. Apparently, when we did this, we crossed into territory not possessed by the United States. None of us knew that. Maybe Lewis and Clark, and maybe the French traders, but not the rest of us. Certainly not me. Very few white men had ever come this far. None of them spoke English.

And a few days later we hit the Bitterroots.

What an odd word. "Bitterroots." Not just a word with two of the same letters together, but three sets of them. It boggles the mind.

If you can't tell, I really don't want to discuss the next month or so. It was not our finest experience on the expedition.

It started out promisingly. A few days in we met the Salish, and Lewis managed to buy twelve horses off of them. We stayed a few days to celebrate with them and their chief, Three Eagles. We knew we were running low on supplies, so we partied very judiciously, and we weren't even hungover the next day.

A word about the variety of natives who have been named after Lewis and Clark shortly after we'd left the tribes behind. It became particularly relevant when we stayed with the Salish. In almost every village we stayed, the leaders offered their young women to us, not as tribute I think, but as a way of getting our blood, fresh blood, into their society. Many of these children were named for Lewis and Clark, but neither of them fathered those children. The captains always refused the women. They gave us permission to indulge, but they never indulged themselves. I could tell it absolutely killed Clark to say no, but no he said. The others, especially the French traders, were very happy to accept such offers.

There was a famous case where a young Salish woman named Clarke was born. It was misspelled, but because Clark was with us everyone thought he was the father. Not so. I suspect the father was Reubin, but I can't be sure.

Missing the whores back home, I often accepted these offers. I got a bit greedy and wound up having sex with two of the women at the same time. Those Salish knew how to please a man, and I hoped that I showed them what my companions were capable of.

We moved on, and when we came to what would be called Traveler's Rest, we decided to camp out. It turns out, according to Old Toby, that this was a popular spot for the natives to camp, usually headed east to hunt buffalo. The way had been rough, so we stayed there because while food was low, we at least had water.

And then we ran out of food. We still had plenty of whisky, which helped a lot of men cope with going hungry, but food? That was gone. And there weren't a lot of animals around for us to hunt.

We moved forward anyway. Morale sank like a rock, and we were all hungry. We had some candles, so a few men ate those. Some men boiled their boots to eat and went barefoot for a while. I wouldn't have recommended that, considering how rocky the terrain was. As a result, their feet got torn to shreds. It wasn't uncommon to see a man leave bloody footprints in his wake.

Most of us started eating the horses. We needed them to get through the mountains, but we had to do it or die of starvation. Since my gear was considerably lighter, I sacrificed my own pack horse. I hated to do it, but I also hated to be crow bait more.

The longer we went, the hungrier we got. Until we met the cannibals. I mentioned them before, right?

We didn't even know until it was too late. As we continued our death march to the sea someone from higher ground jumped down on one of us. It was another French trader we'd picked up along the way. The native, a stringy piece of jerky beef, landed on the back of the trader's horse and bit his neck like a monster. Tore his throat out with his crooked yellow teeth. Keep in mind, I've got bad teeth. For me to say that about someone else is saying something.

Clark was quick with his pistol. As the trader and the native dropped from the horse, Clark whipped around and fired a minie ball into the native's skull. The head came apart at the bridge of the nose and sprayed brains onto the mountain wall so black we couldn't believe it had come out of a human being. Looked like coffee grains.

That's when the rest of the cannibals surrounded us. Going down a narrow canyon, they had met us from the front and the back. Their chief, rail thin with lips so drawn back he looked like a corpse, started talking to us. None of us could understand him, not even Sacagawea and Old Toby. Until the chief pointed to young Pompey. Then we understood very clearly.

"No," Lewis said. "Absolutely not."

The chief understood the tone. He pointed again and made gestures, and I think what he was saying was that if we gave them the baby, they would let us go.

Old Toby tugged on Lewis's sleeve. The following we got from Sacagawea's translation to Charbonneau's translation. She seemed very upset when she said her part, and Charbonneau did not like it one bit, either. "The Nez Perce are maybe two weeks ahead of us. I say we kill these assholes and eat them. That should get us through alive. And if it comes down to it, we can eat the baby ourselves."

We all stood aghast. I couldn't believe that Sacagawea didn't kill the cannibals all herself, not to mention Old Toby, that's how mad she was. Clark reloaded his pistol as quickly as he could, and Lewis turned to Charbonneau. "Tell them that we will let them live if they let us pass without being molested. We will leave their dead companion. They can..." He drifted off a bit, and I could see he was disgusted. "They can eat him."

"What about our guy?" Charbonneau asked. To be fair, I don't think any of us had known his name.

"We will not leave him to these savages," Clark said. "We will give him a proper burial far from this godforsaken place."

Charbonneau spoke with Sacagawea, and she spat his translated words at Old Toby. Old Toby shrugged and made sign with the chief of the cannibals. They seemed to have a difficult time understanding each other, but I think they got their messages through. The cannibals all looked at each other and laughed.

Someone at our back fired. We all turned to see what happened. The cannibals to our backs had been sneaking forward, and Gass had to shoot one of them. They got the message as Gass reloaded his rifle.

The chief looked to Old Toby, and after a bit the translation came through: "These dead men are too skinny. Very little meat on their bones. The baby will be a delicacy. It will fill our bellies until something else comes by. Leave your dead friend, and we might consider it."

"We have the guns," Clark said. "We can take them."

Lewis glanced around. "They have the numbers. And the only gun that doesn't need to be reloaded after each shot is the .46."

"Give it to Hi," Clark said. "He's the best shot. I'll bet he takes down all those assholes behind us. The rest of us? We lay into these guys." He hooked a thumb at the chief. "Get him first. Maybe the rest will flee. Like cutting off the head of a snake."

Lewis considered, and he looked over to me.

"I reckon I can do it," I told him. The .46 was a couple of horses over, in the wagon, but I thought I could get to it quickly.

"Let's kill something," Clark said. "I've been itching to for a while. Lemme scratch."

"All right," Lewis said. "Charbonneau, tell Sacagawea that we're going to trick them. Tell her to tell Old Toby that we're going to give them Pompey. Don't worry, we're not. And she's not to tell Old Toby this. Just convince him that we're doing this. While Old Toby is working on that, I want you, Hi, to get the .46. Do it quietly. As soon as the chief understands, I want you to mow down those bastards back there. The rest of us will attack at the front. Is everyone clear on this plan?"

I had to say, I liked that plan a lot.

We agreed, and as soon as Sacagawea understood and turned to Old Toby, I slipped around the horses to the supply wagon. Lewis made sure that the cannibals at the front were watching him and Old Toby. Clark eyed the cannibals at the back, trying to intimidate them. They took the bait and mocked him. All of them. All their eyes were on Clark. So were their buttholes. They liked to turn and bend over, lifting their loincloths and spreading 'em. They made fart noises with their tongues. From the way Clark grinned, I knew he couldn't wait for what came next.

I set up the .46 in the back of the wagon and lay down on my belly. The others made sure I had a clear path to the group of cannibals, and because it was a covered wagon, they couldn't see what I was doing.

"Now!" Lewis yelled.

The others of our expedition charged the cannibals at the front, and I cut loose at the back. I was supremely lucky. While there were maybe forty cannibals at our back, many of them were lined up, and the bullets were very powerful. So powerful they passed through several cannibals each. I barely had to move the rifle back and forth. I spat death at them, and by the time the twentieth shot fired—the last shot I had—they had about half a dozen men left. I pulled my pistol and expected to get another of them, but they seemed hesitant to make a move.

That was a good thing. I'd left my regular rifle on my horse. I'd only have one shot, and then I'd have to go get the rifle. They could have crossed the space and attacked me with their weapons, which were mostly knifes and spears.

They ran, and I jumped down from the wagon, ready to join the fray at the other side of the skirmish. I didn't need to, though. The cannibals were gone. There had been fifty to sixty on that side, and there were now nearly forty corpses on the ground. One of them was the chief. Someone had shot him through the nose.

The others had fled, too.

Not a single one of our group had been killed.

Sacagawea laughed and jumped up and down, holding Pompey aloft to let him see how she had protected him. Charbonneau couldn't help but grin as he put an arm around his wife's side, still holding a smoking rifle, and touched the child's cheek with his free hand.

"Good work, everyone," Lewis said. "But please reload your weapons. We don't know if they have companions. They may be back."

Old Toby, who seemed to be picking up a little of our language, seemed to understand when he saw us reloading. He got Sacagawea's attention, and the translation eventually came out as this: "Don't worry about those men. They'll be back, but long after we're gone. We've given them plenty of meat."

Lewis grimaced. I think we all did. But we reloaded anyway. I did the same for the .46. Just in case.

Old Toby drew his knife and went to the biggest of the cannibals. He bent down when Sacagawea asked him something. Probably, "What are you doing?"

From the argument that ensued, I'm fairly certain that Old Toby wanted to have a bit of meat for himself.

"I'd sure like to shoot that bastard," Clark said.

"We need him," Lewis said.

"I know. Maybe when we get to the Nez Perce, I'll shoot him."

Considering how things went, maybe Old Toby picked up a bit more than he let on.

We tied the unnamed Frenchman to his horse—his countrymen had already claimed his horse and belongings—and we rode the hell out of that place. Miles down the path we found a place to bury him where the cannibals probably wouldn't find him and dig him up. Since we didn't know his name, we put up a grave marker that said, "Here lyes French trader. Sorry we did naught know yur name." And onward we moved.

We managed to find food here and there. Sacagawea showed us what we could and couldn't eat. It wasn't much, but it kept us alive. We even got to kill an animal once. Scrawny thing, but again, it kept us alive.

A couple of weeks after we saved Pompey from the cannibals, we finally reached the end of the Bitterroots. We camped, and Old Toby outlined to Sacagawea, to Charbonneau, then to us where we would encounter the Nez Perce the next day. Everyone felt very happy. We'd been laying off the whisky because it dehydrated us, and we ran out of water the day before. Now we celebrated, once again wary of our situation. All in all, we only passed two bottles among our party.

The next day was when we found out that we no longer had Toby around. Clark cursed up a blue-streak when he saw that our guide had taken two horses. Lewis cursed, too, just under his breath. Our morale, which had picked up a bit the night previous, suddenly dropped again. Some of us even questioned if Old Toby had told us the truth about the Nez Perce.

But he did tell us the truth. It didn't take us long after we set out that we met with the tribe. Well, Clark and a team went forward while Lewis and the rest broke for luncheon. By the time we caught up to him, Clark had already made friends with the tribe. He'd given them some of the gimcracks we'd brought along as gifts, and they already held them aloft, pleased with their new friends.

We went back with them to their village, which surprisingly lacked men. Most had already gone out east for a buffalo hunt, but the women were very gracious hosts. The hunt was to be the last of the season before the snows came. They had plenty of food, and we all nearly went crazy for dried salmon and buffalo and some kind of odd bread I'd never had before.

We decided to stay for a few days to recuperate and build up our constitutions. And to build more canoes. We had to jettison a few of them while going through the Bitterroots. We also learned how to sew moccasins for the men who had bloody feet from going so long without boots.

Lewis also bartered with them for more supplies, even though we'd been reassured that there would be more game out where we were headed. Like the Shoshone, the Nez Perce wanted guns. This time we didn't trade so much as a pistol. We did get plenty of food, and since we planned on coming back through here on the journey home—it only then occurred to me, with absolute horror, that we'd have to go through the Bitterroots again!—we left a lot of supplies in their care, including a few horses. Naturally, no guns.

I think it was the only time we left a cache with a group of natives during the whole trip.

When everything was sorted out, and we had an idea of what lay ahead, we set out once again, drawing ever closer to the end of our journey.

CHAPTER EIGHTEEN

NOW THAT WE once more had access to reliable rivers, we took to the water again. After navigating the treacherous Quicksand River, Clark pointed out a giant mountain which would be known as Mt. Hood. There were quite a lot of mountains around there. It turned out later, though we didn't know it at the time, that these were actually volcanoes. When the concept was explained to me, it boggled the mind. It made me think of ancient tales from the old country about such things. I'm just glad they didn't erupt while we were there.

Lewis mentioned some of the papers he'd read in preparation for this expedition. Some French explorers had been out in this direction down from New France, and what they'd described sounded a lot like what we were looking like.

"So what?" Clark asked.

"Don't you see?" Lewis beamed like the sun. "We're almost there! We're almost at the ocean!"

That sounded mighty fine to me.

We kept going for a while. I should have mentioned, while we were with the Nez Perce, a native named Twisted Hair had offered his service as a guide of sorts. He was a nice guy and didn't seem to mind doing it for free. Well, and for food and shelter as we made camp several times. He didn't impose, and he helped when he could. I couldn't get a read on him beyond that.

One day he made himself scarce, and the next day he arrived with some bad news. Through the chain of translation, he said, "I'm getting the fuck out of here. Sorry, but you're on your own."

Turned out, he'd done some scouting, and he'd encountered a tribe who had been shadowing us without us knowing it. He didn't know their spoken language, but he figured out their sign. They fully intended to murder us while we slept and take all of our shit.

Lewis tried to convince him to stay and help us, but Twisted Hair refused and that was that. We forged on, but we maintained a higher level of security every night and at the fringes of our expedition every day.

A few days later we found an excellent place to camp. It was at the top of a great hill with many rocks that would protect us. There was also a creek nearby overcrowded with salmon, so we had a steady supply of food and water. We should be safe there. That was Clark's main concern. Lewis's was to contact the tribe and try to make friends.

The first night was spent on edge while many of us found it difficult to sleep, especially now that the tribe—we never did catch their name, or I'm forgetting—no longer thought it necessary to hide themselves. We could see their fires from up on high.

The next day Lewis suggested maybe meeting with them to see if they could communicate and so we could, essentially, do our job. Clark had his misgivings, but they decided to take a couple of canoes and a few men and approach the native camp in midday. This time I was not invited, so I don't really know what happened. York told me later that they'd never seen a black man before, and it kind of awed them. He didn't like being poked and prodded, but he suffered it if it meant that we could make friends of this tribe. Then he said that a lot of them had weird looking heads, mostly the women, like someone put a wood slat on their heads at birth. Flattened, he said. Their heads looked flattened.

I didn't believe that. I thought he was pulling my chain. Nope. When I saw them, I understood what he meant. Like what them Chinese do with their young girls with the foot binding and such.

While the rest of us did odd work, fixing canoes and patching moccasins and such, Lewis and Clark managed to form an uneasy alliance with the tribe. There were a few misunderstandings. When the natives visited us at Rock Fort, which is what we called our camp, tools suddenly went missing. We figured out that the tribe had a policy of payment for services rendered. That was strange, considering that most natives we'd met so far believed the world belonged to all of us. These natives believed this land belonged to them, and that by receiving their help, they were entitled to our tools. It was a rough lesson to learn, especially when Clark killed a goose. The body dropped into the rapids, and a native jumped in, risking his life, to retrieve it for Clark. Clark, knowing now of their policy, just let him keep the dead bird.

So it went until we finally knew that if we left camp for good, the tribe wouldn't follow and kill us.

Maybe a week later, something amazing happened. Or at least that's what we all thought at the time. Still, it boosted morale so much that we almost got into the whisky again, and not just in a moderate amount. We later had to hold ourselves back a bit.

Good thing we did.

Clark saw it first. A beautiful aqua blue glow rising so high that it met the sky and mixed so much we could barely tell the difference between water and air.

In Clark's journal he wrote of the day, "Ocian in view! O! the joy!"

The Pacific Ocean. We could finally see it! We were almost at our journey's end!

So, we celebrated, but we kept it all in. We still had plenty of traveling to do. The next day Lewis scouted out ahead a bit, and by the time we broke for luncheon he came back.

"Bad news," he said. "It's not the ocean. It's actually a large bay. We're close, though. Very close."

It would take nearly two more weeks before we would make it to the end point. Our destination. The beautiful and gorgeous Pacific Ocean. We had to be right this time because we had run entirely out of land.

Lewis and Clark grinned at each other as the entire corps broke out into whoops of joy. We'd done it! We'd made it all the way through!

"Hey, what's that?" Joe Field pointed down toward the very edge of the ocean, where we saw perched on the beach a house with a smoking chimney. Who the fuck could that possibly be? A Frenchman? A Spaniard?

The door to the small house opened, and the crazy bastard we'd seen before stepped out. As soon as he saw us, he screamed. "NO! NO! NO NO NO! WHITE PEOPLE! THESE FUCKS FROM FUCKVILLE FOUND US!"

Us?

He ran back inside. "AMELIA! WE NEED TO GET THE FUCK OUT OF HERE! THE FUCKING WHITE MOTHERFUCKERS FROM FUCKVILLE FOUND US! THEY'RE GOING TO RUIN EVERYTHING! PACK UP! GET EVERYTHING YOU CAN GET!"

"Amelia?" York said.

"Us?" I said.

The lunatic burst out the door again with his arms full of sacks and a cage containing a chicken. He paused and glared at us. "GO BACK TO FUCKVILLE! YOU FUCKING FUCKS!" He then disappeared around the cabin. When he remerged, he dragged a canoe toward the edge of the water. "AMELIA! WE NEED TO FUCK OFF BEFORE THE WHITE PEOPLE GET HERE!"

"WAIT A FUCKING MINUTE!" a woman inside screamed. "I HAVE TO FINISH SOMETHING BEFORE WE GET THE FUCK OUT OF HERE, YOU FUCK!"

They sure did love that word. We'd never seen this Amelia before. He had to have met her somewhere out in this wilderness. I wondered if she was white, too, and if so, what their first meeting was like.

"WE HAVE NO TIME! THE FUCKVILLE FUCKS ARE HERE! THEY'RE WATCHING US RIGHT FUCKING NOW!"

"FUCK YOU, JIMMY! I WILL TAKE MY OWN TIME BURNING THIS FUCKING FUCK HUT TO THE GROUND, YOU FUCK!"

I looked over to Lewis and Clark to see gauge how they were handling this. Lewis stared at the cabin, stupefied, while Clark kept blinking like he thought he'd seen a ghost. York did an imitation of his master, but he wasn't mocking Clark. I don't even think he knew what he was doing.

"AMELIA! RIGHT NOW! FUCK THE STABBIN' CABIN! WE'RE GETTING THE FUCK OUT OF HERE RIGHT FUCKING NOW!"

"IT'S A FUCK HUT, NOT A STABBIN' CABIN, YOU FUCKING FUCK! DID YOU COME FROM FUCKVILLE? HAVE YOU LIED TO ME THIS WHOLE TIME?! SAY IT JIMMY! SAY YOU'RE FROM FUCKVILLE!"

I made a mental note to check any maps for a town called Fuckville. I mean, what were the chances? Then again, the farther you headed out west, the weirder and more vulgar the town names became.

"I'M NOT FROM FUCKVILLE! YOU'RE FROM FUCKVILLE! I KNEW IT!"

By now the windows blazed with flames. More smoke rose up from just under the roof, joining the smoke from the chimney. The door flew off its hinges, and the flames licked out at the lintel. A gruff looking woman with an odd hat that clung close to her head stumbled out, arms full of more supplies. She had spectacles on her forehead. What kind of hat could that be?

"JIMMY! HELP ME WITH THIS SHIT YOU FUCKING FUCK! OR I'LL KICK YOUR ASS BACK TO THE FUCKVILLE FROM WHENCE YOU CAME!"

Jimmy said FUCK a lot more, but he grabbed some of the supplies from Amelia's arms. They threw them into their canoe and launched into the Pacific Ocean. Each grabbed a paddle. Amelia sat in the back while Jimmy took the front. They rowed furiously.

"STOP FUCKING FOLLOWING ME, YOU FUCKS FROM FUCKING FUCKVILLE!" he screamed. "IF I EVER SEE YOU AGAIN, I WILL SEND YOU TO FUCK, THE GOD OF ALL FUCKS FROM FUCKVILLE!" And he kept ranting as they headed for the horizon. We could still hear him across the water even after he'd disappeared from our sight.

"Think we should put that fire out?" Reubin asked.

"No," Lewis said. "It's not worth the effort. It's too far gone, anyway."

We approached the cabin and set up camp while it burned its way out. York approached me, holding something he'd found near the burning ruins. It looked like a card of some sort.

"Hi, you can read. What does this say?"

The top said, "International Brotherhood of Teamsters." If that wasn't confusing enough, there were two sets of numbers. One said "Tel," and the other "Fax." There seemed to be an address of some sort for a place called Washington, DC. Could that mean Washington City? "What the fuck is DC?" I asked.

Lewis took the card from my hand and examined it. "I can only think it means the District of Columbia. Huh. I wonder who this James P. Hoffa is. I've never heard of him."

"Maybe a friend of Tommy Jeff's?" Clark asked.

"That man? A friend of Jefferson's?" Lewis waved a dismissive hand. "I don't know who that insane person was, but he'd never have been tolerated in Washington City, much less at Monticello." He flipped the card into the glowing remains of the cabin, where it burned up almost instantly.

We set up camp, and while most of us celebrated by getting very deep into the whisky, Lewis and Clark had to figure out our next step. They knew that winter was coming, and they had to build a fort for us to stay in until spring. They agreed on that but disagreed on where we should build it. We could stay here, where we'd have plenty of fish. It would keep us alive, but considering an exclusive diet of fish for months on end? It sounded like desperation.

Or we could cross to the other side of the river that had brought us here, which we would eventually call the Columbia River. They gave up trying to figure this one out and tabled it for the evening to join our festivities.

The next day was very rainy, and everyone had hangovers and grumbled most of the time. None of us were happy, and the sight of a couple of natives approaching our camp did nothing to improve our moods. We hoped they were just curious, but we couldn't count on that. If we had to fight, it would probably make our hangovers worse.

Lewis extended the olive branch, and with some translation help we learned that the other side of the river had a lot of elk. The natives—Clatsop, they were called—left us to it, offering no trade.

Lewis took a small team to have a look around. Again, I was not invited, so I don't know what happened. He did return, but he said he didn't see very many elk. So, he and Clark decided to put it up to a vote as to which side of the river we would build the fort. Surprising to all of us, they invited York and Sacagawea to voice their opinions. They got to vote. It was the first—and only—time a slave ever got to vote in our country. It was also the first and only time a woman—a native at that—voted, too.

I have to say, that sounds pretty historical.

There wasn't a contest. We all wanted to cross the river and take our chances there. The next day we moved everything to the other side and began building what would become Ft. Clatsop. Thankfully there were more elk than Lewis had seen, or it would have been a rough winter.

We split the team in two. One would hunt, the other would cut down trees for the lumber necessary to build the fort and the buildings inside. All said, we made good time. That fort was finished in about a month. In fact, we moved in on Christmas Eve. The final touches were put on the next day.

You'd better believe we got into the whisky. Oh yeah. Not too long after that, we met the New Year with a bang. Lots of fireworks and pistols being shot off. Our whisky supply was dangerously low, but we didn't care. We drank as much as we could, and most of us managed to keep it down long beyond reason.

It was one of the best days of our expedition.

So, the months passed. Miserable months. It rained all the time, and it was impossible to be dry. In the meantime, we set up stills to replace our dwindling supply of whisky. We kept all the bottles we'd emptied while at Ft. Clatsop so we could refill them. We refilled them many times, but we were also building up a supply that would get us safely back to civilization. We also made salt from the ocean, which helped make a lot of our blander meals more palatable. We used the time to make about three hundred pairs of moccasins. Those who had suffered the loss of their boots in the Bitterroots swore they'd never suffer like that again.

Not much of note happened during this time, except for one thing. A few more Clatsop natives dropped by, and through our usual translations chain we learned that we'd taken the worst possible path through the Bitterroots. They laughed at us a little, but when they realized the horrors we'd been through, they advised us of a better route to take when going back east.

Why had the Nez Perce not mentioned this to us? I wanted to go back there and strangle them for fucking us over that badly.

But as March began, we started making plans for our return trip. Clark drew maps very well, and he made quite a few while we waited out the winter. We studied these, and we applied the directions that the Clatsop had given us. It actually looked promising. Lewis and Clark even decided to split the expedition so we could get a much better idea of what the fresh American land was like.

We set out for home on March 22, 1806. Our intention was to cross the Lolo Trail, but that didn't happen. Not at first.

Have I mentioned Lewis's dog? I hesitate to do so, but we come to the point of the story where he becomes important, if only for a moment. Lewis loved that dog so much, but he'd given the little fella a very unfortunate name. I know what he meant by the name, but it was a constant joke behind his back. Even I can't help but giggle about it, and I'm an old man now.

It's kind of like farts. Little boys will always find farts funny, and then they grow up and still find farts funny. And then they get old and still find farts funny. Farts, to me, will always be funny.

So, Lewis's dog's name was Seaman.

I had to stop writing because I couldn't stop laughing. Even worse, during the journey to the Pacific, Seaman had been bitten by a beaver. Of all the animals that could have done it, it had to be a beaver!

Even Clark made fun of Lewis over it. When he was certain his fellow captain was out of earshot, preferably on a scouting mission, Clark always made the same joke and giggled at it like the rest of us. "Lewis loves Seaman!"

I should mention that over the course of our journey, when we were starving, we ate a lot of dogs. No one ever touched Seaman, though. Most think it was because we didn't want to harm Lewis's beloved dog. I think, though, it was because no one wanted to be known as a Seaman-eater.

About three weeks after we left Ft. Clatsop, we made camp with a small group of natives. Everyone was starving, but not so bad that we were eating horses just yet. The natives figured we wouldn't mind if they ate Lewis's dog. They didn't know anything about the name, and I wonder if they would have done it had they known.

So, they stole Seaman. They weren't very subtle about it, either. They were getting ready to slit the dog's throat when Lewis found them. He drew down his pistol and aimed it at them. "Give me back my Seaman!" he screamed.

I'd never seen him so furious. At the same time, I did my best not to laugh at what he'd just said. I clutched at my ribs and bit the insides of my mouth, but I trembled with the laughter that absolutely begged to be released.

The natives thought he was kidding, and they moved to cut the dog's throat. "NO!" Lewis yelled. "I will shoot you dead if you so much as harm my Seaman!"

I felt like my head was going to pop, and I could feel my cheeks turn red from the force of holding back my laughter.

Clark's face was red, too. Not with anger, like usual, but with barely contained laughter. He stood by Lewis's side and drew his own pistol. He could barely keep it steady.

The natives got the idea and surrendered Seaman to us.

Sorry. I had to take another break due to laughter. I might have just laughed myself into a hernia.

We eventually made it to the Lolo Trail, maybe a month after the Seaman incident.

God, I must stop laughing.

The Lolo Trail couldn't be passed due to it still being covered with snow. We set up camp and decided to wait out the weather and hope that the Lolo Creek thawed soon. We called it Camp Chopunnish, but I have no idea why.

When we'd still been among the Nez Perce, we made vague plans to meet somewhere around here to get our cache back. We wondered if maybe they were stuck on the other side of the mountains suffering the same conditions. But eventually the cold went away, more or less, and the Nez Perce showed up with our belongings and our horses. Well, most of the horses. They had to eat a few of them. We didn't begrudge them that.

We decided the going looked good, so we began down the Lolo Trail and Creek until we discovered that the core of the mountains was still frozen. We detoured and stayed at Traveler's Rest.

Nothing of note happened during the few days we stayed there. Shortly thereafter we decided to split the expedition. Lewis would lead one team, Clark the other. At the point I need to say that I was chosen for Lewis's team, and I can only vouch for what Clark's team did through several conversations with York later on.

On July 3, 1806 we split the team. Lewis would take his up the Blackfoot River, Clark leading his up the Bitterroot River. Lewis took me, Cruzatte, Thompson, McNeal, both Field brothers, Frazier, Werner, Droulliard and Goodrich. Clark took York, Pryor, Gibson, Hall, Windsor, Ordway, Colter, Gass, LaBiche, Howard, Shields, LaPage, Shannon, Potts, Brattan, Wiser, Willard, Whitehouse and Charbonneau and his family.

Lewis intended to head back to the Great Falls, so off we went. A few days later we crossed that ever historical Continental Divide. A week later, more or less, we made it back to one of our caches. Almost everything was destroyed by weather and time. Our whisky bottles were intact, and we celebrated by opening one of them. We didn't drink much, though. We would need the supply later, and we didn't want to be hungover the next day.

The iron boat seemed intact except for the wood, so we stayed a bit to see if we could patch it up well enough to use. We did an all right job, I think. It only leaked a little.

Then Lewis made a decision I still can't fathom. He decided to split his own group into two teams. I suspect he'd planned this with Clark, considering later events, but I still don't know why he'd want smaller numbers, especially if we met with something or someone dangerous along the way. Lewis wanted to explore the Marias River. He took me, the Field brothers and Droulliard. He left Cruzatte in charge of the others and instructed them to stay at the Great Falls.

So, the five of us went up the Marias. Lewis wasn't as good at Clark with making maps, but he did a fairly good job here. Better than I would have done. It felt kind of odd, us being so few in such undiscovered country, but then I realized that it was just undiscovered by us. A lot of people lived out this way, so they were probably very much aware of this land.

Proof of that came maybe three days into our journey. We set up camp for the night, and for a change Lewis was not restless. Usually, he liked to scout ahead alone, or with one or two others. I think he decided not to do this, considering our small numbers. We ate from our meager supplies, as we couldn't catch or kill anything. As night began to shroud our camp, and I was about to take first watch, we saw fire in the distance.

"What the hell is that?" Joe asked. "Reubin, you got your spyglass?"

Reubin unsheathed it and pointed it into the distance. "I can't see much. I think there are people dancing around the fire, but it could be anything. I can only see shadows."

Droulliard muttered something in French, but he didn't see fit to translate it for the rest of us. I think Lewis might have caught some of it, because he looked over at Droulliard with a puzzled look on his face.

"No," Droulliard said. "Forget I said anything. Forget that fire and those people."

Lewis pursed his lips. "Reubin?" Holding out his hand.

Reubin handed over his spyglass. Lewis looked through it, trying to make sense of what he saw. He just shook his head and handed the spyglass back. "We're heading over there," Lewis said. "Joe, I want you to stay here and guard the camp. The rest of us are going to approach the fire. Very carefully, gentlemen. We don't want to spook them."

"Maybe I should guard the camp," Droulliard said.

"I understood half of what you said. I know you know something about these people. I'll need you more than anyone else."

Droulliard sighed and made sure his rifle and pistol were loaded. Considering that, I did the same. We abandoned our camp and carefully made our way toward the trees, behind which danced the fire, casting shadows everywhere. As we grew closer, we could hear some kind of chanting.

Lewis motioned for us to hide behind the trees as we advanced. We did so, and when we were close enough, he waved for us to stop. I peered around my tree to discover a tribe of...I hesitate to say tribe. These were white people. I knew because they were very much naked, both men and women, dancing around the fire. They wore giant war helmets, and through the eye holes we could see sparkling blue eyes. Their starkly white bodies bore strange markings. Tattoos, I think. They didn't look painted on. Later someone told me that they were runes, whatever those are.

Lewis moved as if he were about to introduce us, but Droulliard grabbed his arm and held him back, shaking his head. Lewis, ever determined, tried to pull away from the Frenchman's grip, but Droulliard wouldn't let go.

Another white man arrived, but this one was bound and hanging upside down. He didn't seem to mind being there. His long blond hair hung like rags from his head as they put a bowl under it. And then they produced a knife.

He offered no resistance, and he didn't cry out, when they slit his throat and bled him out.

I suddenly found myself on Droulliard's side.

So did Lewis. He nodded, and we retreated. By the time we got back to camp we'd explained to Joe what we'd seen. Thankfully he hadn't started a fire yet, so we dug an extra deep pit before doing so. We made sure that the fire didn't rise very much, just enough to keep us relatively warm through the cold night.

Droulliard finally explained himself. "They call themselves Norsemen. They claim to be from Scandinavia."

"Where the hell is that?" I whispered.

"It's near Germany and England," Drouillard said. "About a thousand years ago they were called Vikings. They sailed across the Atlantic in a very primitive boat, and they founded Greenland."

"Where the hell is that?" Me, again.

"It's north and to the east of New France. They say that Christopher Columbus was the first white man to get to the Americas. I think that's bullshit. I think Vikings from Greenland came down here through New France. How else do you explain them?" He hooked a thumb back to the distant fire.

"Have you spoken with them before?" Lewis asked.

"Here and there. Usually, it's just me and one or two of them. But I've learned some of their language. They know more native languages than any fur trader I know, though."

"So it's not wise to start a conversation?" Lewis asked.

"Ever get your throat cut, Captain?" Droulliard asked.

Lewis saw his point.

I stood extra vigilant that night. No whisky for me. And I advised Joe, who had watch next, to not drink, either.

CHAPTER NINETEEN

WE MADE IT through the night unmolested, and we got back in the river as quickly as we could.

Nothing much else happened of note until we reached the end of the Marias River. This frustrated Lewis because he thought there would be more to explore. Instead, we were just tired and aggravated, so we set up camp, which we would call Camp Disappointment. We only stayed the night before heading back in the morning.

The very next day, nearly noon, we saw a tribe of natives by the riverbank. I think they were as surprised to see us as we were them. Lewis immediately had us pull upside of them and onto land. Thankfully Droulliard knew how to speak their language with his hands. They were called Blackfeet. They were very friendly, and we still had enough gimcracks to hand out a few. We decided to split camp for the day so we could learn more about each other. Our numbers evened out a bit. They had eight to our five, but we had guns and they didn't. We figured everyone would be safe.

And that was a bit of a mistake.

It turns out that the Blackfeet's enemies were all those who had been kind to us. Very awkward, to be sure, and Lewis pressed forward, hoping to build a fort out here in an effort to build a relationship with the Blackfeet. He suggested having their chief talk to the chiefs of the other tribes to form a...coalition? I think that's the word. To form a coalition to send delegates to Washington City and work with the American government. He then said something that might not have been the best idea. He said that the other tribes were already on board with this plan. I could see panic in the natives' eyes.

But they remained polite to us.

Lewis and Droulliard kept trying to get through to them, but even so we could tell the going was uphill and through molasses.

We called it quits for the day and went through the usual watch order. I went first, as always. Nothing happened.

I went to sleep, leaving Joe Field to watch. It seemed like I hadn't been asleep long before Joe yelled for us all to wake up. I sat bolt upright under my fur and saw what was going on.

Joe told me later the full story. He'd just woken for his shift, so he still felt sleepy. He knew the risk of falling asleep on duty, so he fought it off as best he could. He saw that the Blackfeet were still crowding around the fire, so he thought it might be wise to be on guard. But he got tired of holding his rifle, so he put it down behind him, close to Reubin's sleeping form.

Rotten luck. One of the Blackfeet managed to sneak up on him and grab the rifle. Still, Joe didn't notice. The act seemed to be a go-ahead order to the other natives, for they snuck into our part of the camp and grabbed Lewis and Droulliard's guns. Why they didn't get to me? I don't know.

But that's when Joe realized what had happened. He screamed for Reubin to wake up, and then for the rest of us. By the time I knew what was happening, Reubin had drawn a giant knife and had given chase to one of the youths who had a bundle of our guns. Reubin, a fast son of a bitch if ever there was one, tackled the Blackfoot native and freed our guns. Then, out of anger, he stabbed the youth in the heart.

We later learned that the Blackfoot was thirteen years old. That still doesn't sit well with me, but at the time we weren't thinking clearly. We fell back into fight or flight, and we fought like hell.

Droulliard shouted something in French. I'd spent enough time with these traders to pick up a few phrases. He said something about his gun to the Blackfoot running off with it.

Lewis sprang up, eyes looking slightly crossed from sudden awareness. He reached for his rifle, but it was already in the hands of another Blackfoot.

"Let me kill this bastard!" Droulliard shouted to Lewis. He had his knife drawn. A big scary skinning knife.

"NO." Lewis went to his saddle and withdrew a pistol he kept there that very few people knew about, hence the reason the Blackfoot hadn't taken it. He chased after the one who had his own rifle and drew down on him. "Stop! Drop that gun!"

The young Blackfoot looked terrified. He quickly dropped the rifle, and Lewis picked it up.

Droulliard had his gun back and held his Blackfoot by the scruff of the neck. By now the Field brothers returned with all of their weapons. They, too, requested permission to shoot these two Blackfeet.

Lewis considered this for a moment. I think he did this because he was still enraged by what he conceived as a betrayal. I considered it that, too, in the immediate time. The more I calmed down, the more I thought about it. The more I saw it from the Blackfeet's perspective. They viewed us as interlopers and friends to their enemies. Why would they not feel threatened by us? Why would they not try to steal our guns?

"No," Lewis said. "Let him go."

Droulliard grimaced, but he released the Blackfoot. Both he and his brother fled to the greater tribe, of which I couldn't help but notice there were considerably more numbers. Had they always been there? Had this been a trap from the start?

And then the Blackfeet turned their attention to our horses. They figured we were distracted, and while we were busy fighting off the gun thieves, they decided to give it a shot. So to speak.

"The horses!" I shouted.

Lewis whirled and saw several young Blackfeet running, leading packs of our horses behind them. Being without guns in the wilderness is one thing. Without horses? We'd be trapped here.

Lewis made the call. "Shoot only the natives with our horses."

We all went one way, and Lewis went the other. Joe, Reubin, Droulliard and I were able to peacefully get our horses back, but Lewis had a different story. He told us later that he'd followed his native until he was nearly breathless. The native then hid behind a rock for a moment. Lewis demanded his horses be returned, and the native jumped out from behind the rock holding a gun. Not one of ours. Lewis said it was distinctly Spanish in style.

He didn't take time to think about it. Instead, he shot the native in the guts. The native, still alive enough to aim, took a shot at Lewis. I read later in Lewis's journal about this incident. He said, "Being bearheaded, I felt the wind of his bullet very distinctly."

The native didn't live long enough for a second shot.

Lewis went a little crazy that day. I'm pretty sure the retreating Blackfeet were just as afraid of us as we were of them, but Lewis took it to a new level. He ordered that by light of the moon, we would get back to the boats with our horses as quickly as we could. While we gathered our belongings and reloaded our weapons and prepared the horses, Lewis gathered up all the weapons the Blackfeet had left behind, including their shields, and threw them into the fire. Some bore amulets, and he cut them off first and kept them. And then he did the craziest thing I'd ever see him do, so completely out of character that I thought Clark might be rubbing off on him.

He took one of the Tommy Jeff medallions and threaded a string of rawhide through it. He draped it around the neck of one of the dead Blackfeet.

We decided to never speak of this again. Lewis had to for his journal. I guess I have to, now, too. Wouldn't be right to leave it out.

We later learned that the Blackfeet banned white people from their lands because of what we did. Can't say I blame them. Remember how I said many of our expedition came to terrible ends? Because of those Blackfeet deaths, one of us later died. George Droulliard, years after we parted ways, came back west to trade more furs. The Blackfeet murdered him.

Anyway, we got to the boats and sailed back the way we'd come. But the time we'd gotten back to the rest of our half of the team, Ordway and Gass had arrived from being dispatched by Clark. They had very little to say in regards to an update. Nothing really happened except they found one of our caches, which turned out to have survived very well. Clark's team once again is replete with tobacco!

CHAPTER TWENTY

THERE IS ONE more thing to relate before our two teams reunited on August 12. It's kind of embarrassing, but it's one of those things that I just can't leave out.

On August 11, the day before Clark and his team met up with us on the Missouri River, something...happened.

It had been a while since we'd had any decent meat, and as we sailed down the river, we spotted elk. A lot of them. Lewis ordered us to the river bank, and he chose Cruzatte to hunt with him. While the rest of us made a temporary camp, mouths watering at the prospect of land meat, the two of them went off.

This is another point where I wasn't there, and I only have Lewis and Cruzatte's stories to rely on. Here is what I know for sure happened.

Lewis had done a good job of sneaking up on the elk we'd passed. He'd taken careful aim at one of them, and just before he fired, someone shot him in the ass. No kidding. In the ass. It hit him so hard he spun, which was good for him. If he hadn't, it would have broken his hip. Instead, he got a giant gash up his flank.

That's what I know for sure. I helped him doctor the injury.

Let me tell you about Cruzatte. He might have known his way around rivers and such, but he was blind in one eye and hard of hearing. The other eye wasn't so hot, either. I don't blame Lewis for a second for thinking that Cruzatte accidentally shot him, thinking he was an elk. Lewis did dress in brown that day.

Lewis told me that he'd screamed at Cruzatte. "Damn you! You've shot me!" And Cruzatte, not being good with hearing things, didn't respond to him. Lewis, thinking that maybe Cruzatte hadn't shot him, suddenly wondered if maybe the natives had made an attempt on his life, so he fled, assuming Cruzatte was behind him. Not so. By the time

Lewis got back to us, and Cruzatte wasn't there, he sent a couple of men to get him.

There were no natives. No sign of them, either. Cruzatte swore upon his own mother's grave that he didn't shoot Lewis, and he seemed so believable. But Lewis had the bullet that bit him. It was a .54, and it was made by the US Army. And Cruzatte, the only other person in the vicinity, carried a rifle that fired .54 bullets.

For as long as I've known him, Cruzatte declared his innocence. Sadly, no one knows where he is now. I knew that the Army still used his services until recently, when it was decided that their maps were good enough and they no longer needed him. For all I know, he's in the room next to mine, dying of old age. But I don't leave anymore. If I were to see him, though, I'm certain he would still deny shooting Lewis.

I did my best to fix Lewis up, but for the rest of the journey, when on the boats he rested front down.

And the very next day, we ran into Clark and his company. Reunited at last!

The captains took to their own counsel as the rest of us celebrated. I gave York a big ol' hug, and we got the last bottle from my private stock. We passed it back and forth, and he told me what he'd been up to in the course of our separation.

He told me what Gass and Ordway had already said. Then things got interesting. In particular, Pompy's Tower. They'd been traveling through a rich valley, and they found a sandstone mound. Clark, possessed by some power York couldn't describe, chose to climb it. When he reached the top, he roared like a bear.

It turns out, maybe mountain lion would be a better analogy. The natives in the area called it "the place where the mountain lion lies."

Regardless, Clark came back down with a breathless story about the beauty he could see for miles on end in every direction. He sang the praises of the land, and I have to say, even now that surprises me. It could be York was padding the story out a bit on behalf of his master, but I don't think so. Every once in a while, a vulgar beast like Clark was capable of moments of beauty.

Clark named it after Pompey. He then signed the Tower with his own name and the date, July 25, 1806.

For some reason, in these modern times, it's been renamed to Pompey's Pillar. Damned historians didn't even get the proper spelling of Jean-Baptiste's name. It's also a shame that so many Americans traveling west now chip out pieces of the Tower for souvenirs, or they want to carve their own names into it. It's a disgrace, but I suppose it's nothing new. People always want a piece of history for themselves.

Shortly after that it was Clark's thirty-sixth birthday. Again, another great celebration. A couple of days later, they were at the place where the Missouri and the Yellowstone met, which was where our reunion was supposed to take place. They abandoned their own camp because the mosquitoes played hell on them.

Around then Clark sent Pryor, Gibson, Hall and Windsor with all of their horses to Ft. Mandan. The way they figured it, they would be able to take boats the rest of the way back to said fort, and they didn't want to have to sail with horses in tow. What happened was, Pryor started noticing that horses went missing. Some one night, some another. And then...all of them. Gone. Despite having set watch, no one knew what had happened.

They did some investigating and found that natives had come in to steal the horses in the dead of night. They were called the Crow, and it's possible that the Blackfeet had warned them about us.

They trailed the Crow for days, and they actually made boats out of bison. I know how crazy that sounds, but I can't deny that it's true. I don't even know how it's done, but they keep the skeleton intact and use the skin to keep them afloat. Regardless, the men were then attacked by wolves, and two of them were bitten. Thankfully the madness didn't come over them, as it sometimes does when a wild animal bites someone.

The funny thing is, Clark had intended to send a letter back east with Pryor asking for government help for the Sioux, as Lewis had discussed with their people. As soon as Pryor and his team caught up, Clark simply gave up on it.

Not too long after that, we were reunited. A few days later, we celebrated Lewis's thirty-second birthday. It was awkward for him, considering he took his repose face down.

And with fresh hangovers we started on the last leg of our journey back to Ft. Mandan.

CHAPTER TWENTY-ONE

LESS THAN A week later we saw Ft. Mandan in the distance, and the Mandan village on the opposite side of the river. A cheer rang out from our men, and we had to restrain ourselves from getting into the last of our homemade booze. As soon as the natives saw us, they let out a series of whoops as we sailed in and docked at the fort. Sacagawea in particular enjoyed showing off Pompey to her fellow villagers. They marveled over how big he'd gotten over the time since they'd seen him last.

And then came the biggest surprise of them all. One of the Mandan women came up to me so happy and proud. It's awkward because I barely remembered her, but when she brought her kids out, I knew that I was the father. It's all in the teeth, I tell you.

One of the twins was a copy of me when I was his age. The other was a goat. The teeth were the same. I wish I'd stayed in contact with them. I wonder where my sons are today. The thought has occurred to me more than once that maybe I should head west just to see them again.

When we returned to Ft. Mandan, we celebrated like there was no tomorrow. We drank and drank and drank and fucked and passed out. Very few of us woke up the next day without our dicks out.

We waited a few days for our massive hangovers to subside. And they were fucking massive. But we weren't home yet. We moved on.

Soon we came back to La Charrette, and Lewis took me aside. "Do you want to stay here?" he asked.

I thought about it. I considered all the people I knew here. I thought about my brother still tending the farm not too far from there. I wanted to see them all again, but at the same time I wanted to be involved with the victory of returning to St. Louis. So, I stayed with Lewis and Clark.

And then they reached the end. It took almost two and a half years.

Tommy Jeff threw us a party. I actually got to meet him. He's not that great. He struck me as very dour and full of himself. He barely trusted himself to drink. Those who don't drink tend to have something to hide. There are exceptions, but Tommy Jeff wasn't one of them.

I did get to meet Aaron Burr. I liked him a great deal, although I didn't expect to. He'd killed Alexander Hamilton a couple of years ago, and I thought him a blackguard. He doesn't like to talk about the duel, but after having spent a considerable time with him—we shared a room during the party, and he didn't even snore—I now think that maybe Hamilton had it coming. Burr is very charming. He agrees with me that slavery is horrible, and he has an odd notion, that I agree with, that women should also vote.

But I spent the most time with York. He was so happy that he'd made it through the entire expedition. We drank and laughed and told each other stories that we both knew very well. It was fun.

I feel bad that Clark didn't grant him his freedom after the journey. If I had enough money, I would have bought him and granted him his freedom. But thankfully York finally got his wish, even if it was many years later.

And then he died of cholera.

A few years after we ended our adventure Sacagawea died of some kind of sickness. No one knows what. Probably cholera. She barely lived long enough to see our second war with the British.

I think I'm the last of the bunch. Gates died a few years back at the age of ninety-nine, so I don't imagine there are any more of us. I can't believe I've lived long enough to see this horrible war between Lincoln and Davis. I should have long been dead. Yet I cling to life, witnessing these disgusting events. If there is any justice, someone will sneak up behind Davis and fire a pistol into the back of his head. I wish Lincoln nothing but the best.

I'm not long for this world. I can't be, can I? I hope not. I'm tired, and I want it all to end. I witnessed the greatest humanity had to offer, and I witnessed the worst. One of my nurses has read this account up until the last few pages, and she suggested that I should find a way to sum everything up.

I can't.

How could I?

AFTERWORD

AND HERE IS where I come out and reveal my true intention in writing this piece. Yes, what you have read is bullshit. Mostly. For those who pay attention to my online rants about finding three sources before accepting something to be true, I have not done so in this case. I played fast and loose with the Lewis and Clark expedition. I know where I wasn't truthful, and I decided to skip it. Why? This is not supposed to be a history book. I wanted to fuck around, so I did. If there is a point in the narrative where you can't help but think, hey, that didn't happen, well, it didn't happen. I didn't want to be beholden to the truth, so I played with it.

But did these things happen? I'd say maybe 30% did happen. I didn't just slip my leash and go barking at a fucking car. I did do some research. Just so that it would at least seem accurate.

Ziege never existed. Too bad. I like the guy. Just about everyone involved in the Corps of Discovery did exist, though. Apologies to them and their descendants.

The reason I wrote this is because of Printer's Row. It's the first lit show I've done. All the others were for comics or horror. But this one honed certain skills that I didn't know I needed.

Those of you who have done shows know how to attract people to your table. But at Printer's Row, it's different. Here's how the common interaction goes.

ME: "How are you enjoying the show so far?"

THEM: "Oh, it's good."

ME: "What do you like to read?"

THEM: "Oh, you know, I like to read everything."

ME: (simmering, knowing that I like to read everything, but you're not helping me) "Cool. Me, too. What are you reading now?"

THEM: (90% of the time) "Oh, I'm reading a biography. I love biographies."

ME: (looking at our horror and bizarro table, knowing there are no biographies) "Uh, *Fox News Fuck Fest* by Mandy De Sandra is based on the true story!"

Which, by the way, really happened. I tried to sell that book as a biography. But the simple fact of the matter is, when you're at Printer's Row, very few people are there for fiction. They want nonfiction. They want (auto)biographies. By the nature of our business model, we don't have those.

So...why not make one up? I suggested we do a round robin type of biography, and my fellow bizarros laughed and enjoyed the idea, but no one wanted to do it. So fuck it. I did it. You're holding it in your hands right now.

Thank you for reading this. I know it's slightly duplicitous in that I probably sold you on it pretending it was an autobiography that I brought back from the mists of time, but I hope you get the joke and are laughing with me and not at me.

But.

Well.

Who knows? It could have happened.

Love and kisses,

JOHN BRUNI

ABOUT THE AUTHOR

JOHN BRUNI lives in, until he is legally convicted from, Elmhurst, IL, where he promises he loves history and everything that comes with it.